THE ADVENTURES
OF
RICKY AND CHUB

THE ADVENTURES OF RICKY AND CHUB

By MYRTLE SHAY

Illustrated By
PAUL E. KENNEDY

LANTERN PRESS, INC. · NEW YORK, N. Y.

29080

Library of Congress Catalog Number 65-19354

PUBLISHED SIMULTANEOUSLY IN CANADA BY
GEORGE J. MC LEOD, LTD. TORONTO

MANUFACTURED IN THE UNITED STATES OF AMERICA

TABLE OF CONTENTS

THE ADVENTURES
OF
RICKY AND CHUB

INTRODUCTION

Viewing our country today, with its network of super-highways and cars zipping along over them, with its airplanes and jets flying faster than sound, and its astronauts probing the heavens, it is hard to realize that less than a hundred years ago, there were none of these things. Within the memory of some folks living today, much of this land of ours was still unsettled, with vast areas in wild timberland.

In the 1870's, when the pioneer boys, Ricky and Chub Bonifield, lived with their parents in a section of central Indiana called the Hawpatch, the surrounding country was still sparsely settled. There was much wild game in the timberland. Trappers lived in crude cabins along the Hawcreek and White Rivers. And, now and then, a belated covered wagon moved westward behind slow oxen in search of a new home.

Instead of the broad paved highways we have today, there were only rutty trails, except for a few gravel roads, called pikes, linking the larger towns. Folks traveled mostly on horse-back, although buckboards and spring wagons were also much in use during those months when vehicles could follow the trails without getting stuck in the mud or caught in deep snowdrifts. Often neighbors were miles apart and there were no telephones by which to call for help if someone were in trouble.

The men and women of those days were hardy, sober, and industrious. Little red school-houses had, for the most part, replaced the log cabin structures of earlier days. Because of the distance between the homes of the settlers, many of the children had to walk two or three miles through the timber to go to school and learn their reading, writing and arithmetic.

Life was crude and the pioneers endured many hardships. Boys of twelve or thirteen years of age were often called upon to do a man's work. On the farm, boys were expected to feed and water the livestock, do the milking, plow the fields, and to help plant the grain as well. There were trees to be felled; there was wood to be chopped, grain to be carried to the mill for grinding into flour and corn meal. Boys attended school only when they could be spared from the work on the farm. No boy of those days could ever complain that there was nothing to do.

So, with an understanding of the times in which they lived, let us now join the group in the old farm house and meet Ricky and Chub in their Hawpatch Valley home.

1. DEAD OF NIGHT

Snuggled down in our warm feather bed, my twin brother, Ricky, and I counted the strokes as the clock on the mantel downstairs bonged ten times. We heard the bronze chains of the hanging lamp go "ga-rumph!" as Father pushed it all the way up to the ceiling. That meant he had finished reading the Hawpatch Weekly, and that he and Mother were getting ready for bed.

We could hear Father scraping up ashes from the hearth to bank the fire. Then, Mother came up the stairs, the light from the lamp she carried flitting ahead of her. For a moment, I could see the speckles on Ricky's snub nose and the wisp of straw-colored hair that always seemed to be trying to run away.

Father was still puttering around downstairs when Jake, the hired man, came in. It was Saturday night and he'd been to town as usual. His voice, high-pitched with excitement, carried up the stairs. "Fannie Bell's been stolen!" he cried. "She wasn't in her stall when I put up my horse."

Fannie Bell! Ricky and I sat up with a jerk. My heart felt like a piece of lead pipe and it was poking a hole in my stomach. Fannie Bell gone! She couldn't be! She just couldn't!

Fannie Bell was our horse, Ricky's and mine. We'd claimed her ever since she was born. That day, we had coaxed her away from old Mollie, and she came and rumpled against us while we stroked her. She was all fuzzy and soft and red, except for a white spot on her back, and her mane was like a flame when she ran with the wind. She would come to us when we whistled, and we were riding her bareback long before she'd been broken to harness.

We waited miserably, hearing the sounds downstairs; Father taking down his muzzle-loader; Jake shuffling around.

After awhile, they went out, carrying the lantern, and we watched the light go bobbing off around the barn to the stable. We caught shadowy glimpses of Father and Jake on their horses, then the lantern was put out and we heard the horses go galloping clippetty clop down the pike.

Ricky was clutching me and his hands felt cold and sticky. "What'll we do, Chub? What'll we do about Fannie Bell?" he wailed.

There didn't seem to be much that two thirteen-year-old boys could do. We huddled under the quilts, stunned by our loss. I had an awful lump in my throat and the darkness was smothering me. I could feel Ricky's shoulders quivering and I knew he was crying inside just the way I was. Being identical twins, Ricky and I not only looked alike, but we felt the same way about most things, especially about Fannie Bell.

I tried to cheer him. "Aw, she'll come back,"

I said, though I knew she wouldn't—unless—
unless—the thought staggered me—unless we
went looking for her! I poked my brother.
"Ricky," I said, "we've got to find Fannie
Bell. If she's near, she'll come when we whistle; if she's tied, she'll neigh."

"But, Chub," Ricky protested, "horse thieves
are killers. Father said so. Maybe they'll kill
us."

"We won't get caught," I said stoutly,
though I didn't feel very brave.

Ricky was pulling on his trousers. "I'll bet
Fannie Bell's down in the bottoms some
place," he declared shakily.

The bottoms! A shiver ran up my spine.
Father had warned us many times not to go
into the wild timberland along the river. Jake
had shot a panther in the woods only the week
before, and we'd heard him say it had probably
come up from the river bottom. "We—we—
we—can't go in there in the dead of night,"
I sputtered.

Ricky reached across the bed to grip my arm.
"Dead of night or no dead of night, we've got

19

to," he whispered. "We've got to save Fannie Bell."

I fumbled for my clothes and put them on. We slipped down the back stairs and out through the kitchen door.

We floundered along through the patches of dirty snow left from a recent thaw, until we came to the rail fence zigzagging the edge of our farm, and climbed over. Ahead of us lay the timber that ran into the bottoms. There was a full moon coming up. Pretty soon, we could see everything near us; the timber standing out black, with the big red moon behind it; the crooked rail fence with the haw trees tight in its corners, and the little patch of clearing where the fence ended with black shadows all around. There was a wild dampish smell of heavy timber, with the night mists washing the pines. We stopped.

Ricky's hand gripped mine. "It's—it's—just like going into a cave," he said fearfully. "Are—are you scared, Chub?"

My knees felt shaky, and my teeth clicked

so it was hard to talk. "Let's whistle," I said.

Ricky gave the familiar call. Standing close together, we listened. But not a sound came back on the icy air. Only the hovering silence of black wilderness waiting to swallow us.

I was shaking from head to foot. Icy fingers slithered along my spine. "Let's—let's—go—home," I chattered. "We'll ge-e-e-t lost in there."

Ricky began to whimper. "But—but, Chub," he quavered, "we'll never see Fannie Bell again unless we find her to-night."

"We'll call once more," I said. I pursed my lips and whistled as loudly as I could. We waited. Then, suddenly out of the night there came the plaintive, far-off neighing of a horse.

"She's in there, just like I told you," Ricky cried. "Come on!"

The blackness grabbed us as we reached the timber. Holding tight to each other, we went in. Something thudded to the ground behind us. I jumped and my skin crawled. "Maybe it's a—a—a—panther," I choked. We cowered against a tree and waited. Nothing happened.

Ricky's breath was hot on my cheek. "Cl—cl—clubs!" he stuttered.

We groped around on the ground with our mittened hands. With the sticks for weapons, we went on, jumping half out of our skins at every sound. When we stopped again, the river was almost at our feet. I whistled. A neigh, so close it startled us, came back.

"She's close, Chub!" Ricky gloated.

"Sh!" I cautioned.

We followed a little path along the bank for a way, then we had to fight the brush again. Ricky was in front. Suddenly, he stopped short and squeezed my hand. Just ahead, in a little clearing, the moonlight streamed down upon a sorrel mare with a white patch on her back. She was tied to a sapling. No one was with her.

Fannie Bell! I started toward her. Ricky pulled me back. "Somebody may be hiding," he cautioned.

We crept along the edge of the clearing until we reached the sapling. Fannie Bell whinnied softly as we approached. She nuzzled our hands as we stroked her. I tried to unfasten the rope, but the knot was so tight I couldn't budge it. Then, I tried to cut the rope with my knife, but the blade was dull and the rope thick. I had cut it only half through when a sound from upstream sent us scurrying into the brush.

We heard the lapping of oars and presently a rowboat pulled into shore. Two men got out and scrambled up the bank. They were huge, black-bearded men and one of them lunged when he walked.

Crouched in the shadows, too frightened to move, we watched them lead Fannie Bell down the bank to the river, urging her into the water, while she pulled hard against the rope. As they settled themselves in the boat, I began to understand. The brush was too thick to lead a horse through it in a hurry. They could make better time by boat, forcing the horse to swim.

Ricky was half sobbing. "Chub," he whimpered, "they'll get away and we can't do a thing to stop them."

One of the men had the oars and the other

was trying to force the mare into the water. Fannie Bell planted her feet solidly in the bank and held on.

"Let go there, you blasted filly," the man roared, giving the rope a jerk.

Fannie Bell didn't budge. The oarsman struggled to get the boat out into the current. "You've got to jolt that mare loose," he growled.

His companion stood up in the boat. "Let's see you do it," he grumbled. "I'll row."

Ricky and I were hiding in the fringe of trees almost in the water. I was so close to Fannie Bell I could have reached out and touched her. Both men were standing up in the boat, changing places. If only Fannie Bell would suddenly jerk and capsize the boat! Quick as thought, I swung my foot and kicked her hard in the flank.

The mare leaped straight into the air. Then suddenly she reared back on her haunches. The half-cut rope had broken, capsizing the boat and throwing both men into the water.

24

We could hear them splashing about and cursing.

Fannie Bell tore around the clearing like mad. Suddenly she came straight at us. We scrambled to one side and I managed to grab the rope. "Whoa there, Fannie Bell! Whoa, old girl!" we soothed.

In a moment, she quieted down and let us lead her, but we were in for trouble. We hurried as fast as we could, but leading a horse through the heavy brush was slow work. We had gone about thirty feet when Ricky whispered: "If we can only get to the foot path, we'll make it."

The thieves were out of the river now, their angry voices coming nearer and nearer, as they fought their way through the brush. Ricky's words rang in my ears: "Horse thieves are killers. Father said so."

"Ricky," I whispered, "we'll have to let Fannie Bell go."

"No, we won't." My brother stopped. I couldn't see him, but I knew his blue eyes were flashing like they always did when he got stubborn. "We'll get on Fannie Bell and head right into them. We'll be in the river before they can stop us."

We turned the mare around and climbed up on her back, Ricky in front. "When we get almost on them, you kick Fannie Bell in the flank," he ordered.

The men were getting closer. On they came, yelling and crashing through the brush. Another minute, and Ricky lifted his head from the mare's neck. "Now!" he whispered hoarsely.

I kicked with all my might and clung to Ricky. I thought for a moment that Fannie Bell was going to throw us. She took that brush like a cyclone. The men leaped aside as we shot past them and out into the clearing. There, Fannie Bell tried to stop short and we almost went over her head.

Fearfully, I looked back. One of the men came lunging across the clearing right behind us. Another second and he'd rake us off the

The men leaped aside as we shot past them . . .

horse. My heart popped into my throat. Ricky screamed in my ear: "Kick her, Chub! Kick her!" But my legs were stiff. They wouldn't move. I tried to kick and couldn't.

Then, everything happened at once. With a roar of triumph, one man grabbed the halter. The other grabbed Fannie Bell's tail. If there was anything that made Fannie Bell mad, it was having her tail pulled. Her hind feet shot out and I bounced up and down on her back with a jolt that loosened my wits. I kicked. The mare leaped, snorting. The man hanging onto the halter let go with a yell, and the next instant we were in the river. For a moment, the water swallowed us. Then we were bobbing along on the surface, wet to the skin, but safe on Fannie Bell's back.

Down the river a way, we guided her up the bank to the foot path and coaxed her into a lope. It was hard going when we left the path to cut across the timber, but we knew the horse thieves couldn't catch up with us now.

We reached home just as Father was coming

in from the barn with his lantern. When he saw us, his jaw dropped. "What sort of tom-foolery is this?" he thundered. "Where'd you boys have that horse hid?"

I thought for a moment he was going to thrash us right there. "This isn't any tom-foolery," I flared. "We found Fannie Bell in the bottoms and brought her home."

After that, Father didn't say much. He didn't even scold us for going into the timber. When we'd told him all about it, he took his muzzle-loader and went out, looking grim, and we knew he was going to rout Jake out of the lean-to for a new man hunt.

Mother gave us hot milk to drink and sent us to bed. But we couldn't sleep. We lay there listening to the elm trees brushing the eaves, and feeling the cold air from the window whipping across our faces. The darkness came in close. It smelled tangy and damp like the pines. But it was a friendly sort of darkness, not the smothery kind.

Ricky squeezed my hand under the quilts

and I knew he was feeling glad all the way down inside him like I was, for his palm wasn't cold and sticky now. It was warm and soft like the tip of Fannie Bell's nose.

2. NIGHT WATCH

Ever since we first heard a panther scream, Ricky and I had been mimicking the terrifying cry that had frozen our blood that night. We were pretty good at it too, especially Ricky. He could let out with a yowl that would make you think a panther was right there on top of you.

Jake had shot the cat, stuffed the hide and put glass eyes in the head. He wanted to keep it in his room, but Mother wouldn't have it in the house, so he stored it out in the cabin where we kept the buckets and kettles we used at maple sugar time. Ricky and I liked to go out there to play with the stuffed panther while we practiced our yowling.

That's what we were doing that Saturday afternoon in early March, while Father and Jake were tending the kettles of maple sap they were boiling down into syrup. There were three kettles swung over open fires in a little clearing near the shed, which was an eighth of a mile or so from our house. All around was a heavy forest of timber.

We heard Father tell Jake he'd have to go into town that night, and since Jake always took Saturday night off, there wouldn't be anyone to watch the syrup while it was cooling after the boiling was done. Ruffians from outside the neighborhood sometimes came in and rebuilt the fires under the kettles, boiling all the syrup down into sugar, eating what they wanted and scattering the rest through the snow. Father had lost his syrup that way one winter. Since then, he'd always kept watch.

"I'll just have to take a chance on it tonight," he worried.

"Well, I'd be glad to stay if I hadn't promised Elvira I'd be over," Jake said. "I'd hate to disappoint her."

"Yes, of course," Father agreed. "You go ahead and see your girl. Most likely nobody'll bother."

Ricky nudged me. "We could keep watch," he declared.

"Of course, we could," I echoed. "Let's."

Together, we ran outside to tell Father. Jake scoffed at the idea. "What could you young ones do against a half dozen bullies?"

I wavered. Thinking about it that way, I wasn't so sure I wanted to keep watch. But Ricky stood his ground, his face flushed with excitement. "I bet you we could scare them off, even if there were a dozen," he boasted.

I couldn't let Ricky down, so I chimed in: "Of course, we could," though down inside me, I was wondering just how we'd go about doing it. I felt a little sick at my stomach as Father took up for us.

"Well, Jake," he said, "I've always held that two half-grown boys ought to equal one grown man, and I reckon if they think they can do a thing, they can. We'll give them a chance, anyway." Then to us: "Better get your chores done early so you can be here by dark."

Ricky looked like he wanted to snap his suspenders for pride, only he couldn't because his overcoat covered them up. Seeing him so sure of himself made me a little ashamed of the quavery feeling inside me. I knew my brother didn't have any more idea what we'd do than I did, but you just couldn't scare Ricky until he was right in the middle of the scare.

We were back at the kettles by dusk. The syrup was all done and the fires under the kettles had been put out. Our job was to see that no one rekindled them to boil the sap into sugar for "tasting and wasting," as Mother would have said it.

We built a fire of dead sticks to keep us warm and sat down on the horse blanket Father had spread on the snow. The woods grew darker, and strange scary sounds kept us aquiver with excitement. We sat there staring into the fire and jumping half out of our skins every time a twig snapped.

34

We'd been out there a couple of hours and I was wishing we were home in bed, when, all at once, a sound reached our ears that didn't belong to the woods. It wasn't an animal sound and it wasn't the wind. It was more like a blast from a trumpet, muffled and far away.

"Wha-at was that?" I quavered, clutching at Ricky.

"I—I—don't know," he whispered. "What did it sound like to you?"

Before I could answer, it came again from the woods back of us toward the river.

Ricky jumped to his feet. "Let's get out of the firelight," he said. "Let's get behind the sugar house and wait."

We darted off into the woods and circled back, like Grandfather had told us they used to do in Indian times. Behind the cabin, we stood close together against a giant oak tree that spread its branches far above the shed. We stood there a long time. We were getting cold and I was thinking that maybe we were just fraidy cats and ought to go back to the fire, when suddenly Ricky grabbed my arm and pinched it so hard it hurt.

"What's that coming out of the woods?" he faltered.

I couldn't see anything. "Where?" I choked.

Ricky was frantic. "There! There!" he whispered, pointing, "right at the edge of the clearing!"

I looked again and my heart jumped right into my throat. The thing coming toward us was big and shapeless and blacker than the sky. It pitched from side to side with a sort of shambling gait. Its eyes looked like bright red coals set about two feet apart, and they kept blinking in the most unearthly way.

Ricky made a sound like he was choking. "Up!" he blubbered, and started climbing the tree.

I was stiff with fright and my legs wouldn't take hold of the tree trunk, but my brother shinned up like a monkey. "Hurry!" he urged, and caught my hand, helping to pull me up.

Up among the branches, our dark clothes almost the color of the tree, we could see what was going on around and beneath us, without much danger of being seen. We looked back at the spot where the thing had been that scared us, but it was gone.

"What do you suppose it was, Ricky?" I whispered.

"I don't know, but I'm glad we're up here instead of on the ground," he said.

We were both shaking from fright and from the cold. Our fire still burned, but it was getting low. Several minutes passed without further sign of the monster, and I was beginning to wonder if it wouldn't be a good idea to climb down and run for home, when, there across the firelight on the other side of the clearing, we saw the thing again. It came plunging and floundering toward the camp, its fiery eyes blinking, now one, now the other. Ricky grabbed me and I clung to him, staring in terror at the frightful black shape coming nearer and nearer.

It was just outside the circle of light from our fire when, all at once, it reared like an elephant getting ready to stamp with his front feet. Then it sort of pitched forward on the ground, and suddenly there wasn't any monster any more, but three men with a lantern. They rushed up to the fire, yelling and laughing, and dragging an old buffalo robe.

We couldn't see who they were until they piled more brush on our fire and made the flames leap high. Then we made out they were three trappers, who lived in a shanty up the river.

Ricky pinched me. "The thing was only a buffalo robe thrown over them, with holes for eyes, and a lantern," he whispered.

I didn't say anything, for right then one of the men started talking. "I thought Jake said Bonifield's young ones would be watching tonight," he sneered.

Another man pointed to the blanket we'd left by the fire. "They've been here," he said, "but I reckon we scared them and they went home."

"Scared easily, didn't they?" the third man put in. He tossed an old trumpet onto the blanket.

I nudged Ricky. "That's what we heard," I whispered. I was so mad I was choking. It was bad enough to be scared half to death, but to have it turn out to be a prank and to hear the men making fun of us was too much. Ricky's hand gripped my wrist till his nails cut me, so I knew he was just as mad as I was. There wasn't a thing we could do about it, either. We just sat and watched while they gathered brush and began piling it under the kettles.

"I'd like to see Bonifield's face when he finds what is left of his sugar," said one, and they all laughed loudly, like it was a big joke to ruin Father's syrup.

"We've got to do something," I whispered. "We can't let them spoil all that syrup." I started to grope my way down to the crotch of the tree.

"What are you going to do?" Ricky asked.

"I'm go-o-ing down and ma-a-ke them pu-u-t out tho-o-se fi-i-res," I chattered. "And I'm go-o-ing to tell tho-o-se men wha-a-t I think of them."

Ricky pulled me back. "Wait!" he rasped

39

close in my ear. He clambered over me and started down.

"Where are you going?" I questioned.

Ricky lay forward along the limb, his face close to mine. "The stuffed panther," he whispered.

Then, I knew what he was going to do, and my heart thumped with new hope. But before I could say anything, he had slipped away down the tree. I started to follow him when my coat caught on a twig. By the time I'd got myself loose and started to slide down again, Ricky was back, half dragging the stuffed panther. I reached down and pulled it up into the tree.

Just behind the cabin ridgepole, where the shadows were thick, he gave my coat a tug, so I knew he wanted to stop there. Together, we edged the stuffed hide over the ridgepole. Holding on to the tail, we let the body slide down the steep roof, so that the light from the fires would make the glass eyes shine.

"I'll hold the tail," I offered.

"Keep him moving," Ricky cautioned.

He straightened up a little behind the ridge-pole. "Now!" he whispered, and I gave the panther hide a jerk to make it wriggle like it was alive. Then I almost tumbled out of the tree as the horrible wailing cry splintered the night silence.

The men jumped like rabbits. For an instant they stared at the crouching form on the roof, their eyes popping with fright. In my excitement, I let go of the panther's tail, and he hurtled down the steep roof toward the men. With a wild yell, they streaked for the woods. It was lucky for us that they were too scared to look back and see our panther crumpled on the ground.

There were three caps, a lantern, an old horn and several mittens lying on the ground about the kettles when we got down. We put out the fires under the kettles, carried the panther back to the shed, and dragged the buffalo robe and our horse blanket to the edge of the timber. We spread the robe down behind a thicket and huddled together under the blanket.

41

"I bet they don't come back," Ricky snickered. "But, if they do, we don't want them to find us."

"We'll get back and build our fire before Father gets here," I declared. "And we won't let on how scared we were."

But we didn't wake up until the sun was pretty high and we heard Father shouting: "Ricky! Chub! Where are you?"

He sounded real scared too, till he saw us coming. Then, he started to bluster like he always did when he found us safe after one of our escapades. "What do you mean, leaving the fire and going to sleep?" he roared. "And what are those caps and mittens and this lantern and horn doing here?"

"That's what's left of the men who tried to steal the syrup," cried Ricky.

Father's jaw dropped. "Wha—at's that?" he demanded.

Ricky gave me a look that meant I was to keep still. His chest swelled with importance. "Oh," he said lightly, "those three trappers

42

up river tried to steal the syrup, but we scared them away."

Father looked from one of us to the other. "What did you do?" he asked.

We had to tell him then, only we didn't say anything about our being scared. When we had finished, Father just laughed and laughed like he was fit to burst, and when we got home and went in the house to tell Mother, he was still chuckling softly to himself.

3. THE GOLD HUNT

The wagon wheels went crunching the light crust of snow. "Going on a gold hunt! Going on a gold hunt!" they sang, with Danny's hooves beating the time. The words were plain as anything to Ricky and me, but Uncle Joe couldn't hear them.

My brother and I were perched on the wagon seat up front beside Uncle Joe Bascomb, and we were wishing that we were going on a gold hunt too, instead of just as far as our Aunt Sarah's, to visit until Uncle Joe picked us up on his way home. But Father had said we were too young to go on a wild goose chase, hunting gold in the hills.

Uncle Joe was staying with us that winter. He was a jolly little fellow, with a fringe of gray hair around the rim of his bald head, a chubby nose, and blue eyes that twinkled a lot. He had one gold tooth right up in front, and it always gleamed in the firelight like it was happy to be there, peeping out of Uncle Joe's mouth.

As we rode along, Uncle Joe showed us the gold finder he'd bought from Sam Snyder, who owned the Hawpatch general store. It was a little piece of wood with two prongs at one end. "I gave Sam two dollars for it," Uncle Joe said, "but it'll take the work out of prospecting. Sam says it'll stick to any rock with gold in it."

That night we spent with a trapper named Owens, and the next evening, we reached Uncle Aaron's farm. But when we drove up the lane to his log cabin home, we found the place deserted. "Looks like they've moved away," said Uncle Joe.

45

Ricky pinched me. "Now, we'll get to go on the gold hunt," he gloated.

For a moment, Uncle Joe just stood there like he didn't know what to do. Then, all at once, he was beaming at us and we knew everything was all right. "Well, boys," he said, "I guess this fixes your visit with your Aunt Sarah."

"We don't care," we chorused. "We'd rather go with you on the gold hunt."

We built a fire in the fireplace, cooked our supper, and made up our beds on the floor. Next morning, we were up long before daylight and by sunrise we were huddled on the wagon seat alongside Uncle Joe, with the buffalo robe tucked around us and old Danny clopping along over the frozen trail. It was almost dark that evening when we pulled up in front of a shack on the bank of a little creek.

"Well, here we are, boys!" Uncle Joe cried cheerily. He grabbed the axe and set about cutting pine boughs for our beds, while Ricky and I gathered brush for fire. With beds made, our supplies inside, and a stack of wood by the door, Uncle Joe soon had the flames leaping in the fireplace and our supper cooking in the long-handled skillet.

The next day was clear and cold. "Just the weather for prospecting," Uncle Joe declared. He made us some flapjacks for breakfast and then we set out, following the river up-stream; Uncle Joe with the gold finder, and Ricky and I carrying the pick and shovel and a burlap bag to put the gold in.

Whenever we'd come to a place with outcroppings of rock along the bank, Uncle Joe would scramble down into the creek bed and try out his gold finder. He'd go tapping along the rock with it, and when it didn't stick to the rock, he'd shake his head and clamber back up the bank. We put in the whole morning that way, and, by noon, Uncle Joe was looking whipped. But, after we'd eaten the cold flapjacks we'd brought with us, he took up the gold finder again.

"We'll try the ridges," he said, and started up the hill in a trot.

For several days, Uncle Joe prospected in

47

the hills, without finding anything. Then, one morning, we got up to find the sky sagging down, dark gray and angry looking. Uncle Joe hustled us out right after breakfast for wood to stack outside the door. He kept us gathering brush most of the day, while he chopped the heavier logs into proper lengths for the fireplace.

The sky kept getting darker all the time and the clouds were churning around like they wanted to get started but something was holding them back. Toward evening, Uncle Joe took his muzzle-loader and went out looking for rabbits. "We may get snowed in," he said, "and some fresh meat will come in handy."

After he'd gone, Ricky and I fed and watered Danny and made his stall as tight as we could. We nailed some boards over the broken windows of the shack, piled more logs on the fire and sat down to wait for Uncle Joe.

"I hope he brings home a rabbit," Ricky said longingly. "I'm tired of side meat."

"I could eat a whole rabbit, myself, right

now," I declared. I got up and went outside
to see if Uncle Joe was in sight, and then I
forgot all about rabbits for supper. It was dark
now, and just as I opened the door, a big
feathery snowflake settled on my nose. The
storm was on us and Uncle Joe hadn't come
home. In a snow storm, he'd never find the
cabin. I went back to the fire. "Ricky," I said,
trying to keep the fright out of my voice,
"we've got to help Uncle Joe."

My brother looked up, startled. "Why?" he
asked.

"It's snowing," I explained. "Uncle Joe
won't be able to find the cabin if the storm
thickens."

Ricky was on his feet, his face anxious.
"What'll we do, Chub?"

"Let's light the lantern and hang it in the
window," I suggested. "Maybe he can see it
if he gets anywhere near."

We hung the lighted lantern at the top of
the window, and then we went outside to look
at the storm. The snow was coming down

faster now, swirling in great feathery rolls. The ground was already white. The lantern cast a feeble light. It wouldn't carry far.

Ricky was staring off into the darkness, his chin thrust forward. I saw his shoulders straighten. "Chub," he quavered, "we've got to go after Uncle Joe."

My teeth were chattering from fright. "I know we have," I said, "but we don't even know which way he went."

"And how will we find our way back?" Ricky wailed.

All at once, I remembered a big ball of very heavy twine that Father kept in the wagon to mend the harness when it broke. "We'll fasten the end to the cabin door," I said. "Then we'll take the ball and let it unwind as we go, so we can follow it back."

Ricky was already halfway to the wagon for the twine. We tied the end securely to the door knob and pushed a stick through the ball for a spindle.

"We'll take the lantern," said Ricky, "and the axe."

"We'd better take Danny too," I said. "If the string breaks, maybe he'll know the way back."

The storm swirled white and thick around us as we set off across the clearing. Every few steps we'd stop and shout and listen and swing the lantern high, but all we heard was the howl of the wind.

When we reached the woods, we had to be careful so the string wouldn't catch in the brush. Ricky went ahead, leading Danny and carrying the lantern. The axe was strapped on Danny's back. I followed, letting out the string. On and on we went, shouting at the top of our lungs: "Uncle Joe! Uncle Joe!"

After awhile, we were so hoarse our voices sounded like fog horns, but we kept on. All at once, the stick I was holding gave a little jerk. I grabbed for the ball of twine. It wasn't there. My heart jumped. The twine had run out. Maybe we couldn't find it! I shouted to Ricky. He hurried back with the lantern. After a frantic search, we found the string lying on the snow.

"What'll we do now?" I wailed.

"We'll go back," Ricky decided sensibly. "You wind up the string and when we get to the cabin, we'll start off in another direction."

Back at the cabin, we warmed ourselves and considered our next move.

"Let's follow the creek," I suggested.

"We might as well," Ricky said gloomily. The snow was falling steadily when we started out again. We trailed the string behind us, swinging the lantern, and yelled and yelled until the twine ran out again. We stood there in the flickering light of the lantern, with old Danny hanging his head and wanting to go home, and a lump came up in my throat that I couldn't swallow. Ricky was feeling the same way, I guess, for suddenly we were clinging to each other and crying just like babies. "Uncle Joe's dead," I sobbed. "He—he's dead."

All at once, Ricky stopped crying. He straightened up, clutching my arm. "Did you hear that?" He cupped his hands around his mouth and shouted: "Uncle Joe!"

And then, I heard it too—a faint cry of "Help! Help!" coming from far down the creek. Without another thought of the twine, we started running, scrambling over rocks and fallen timber, pulling old Danny in a trot behind us.

The cries for help kept getting nearer and pretty soon we could hear Uncle Joe's voice close by, but we couldn't see him anywhere. Then he called, "Here! Here!" and, with the lantern, we made out a pile of brush partly covering a deep pit. Uncle Joe was down in the bottom, lying there and groaning something awful.

We pulled the brush away and scrambled down beside him. His face was twisted with pain. "It's my ankle," he groaned. "I think it's broken. I fell into this blasted bear trap and couldn't climb out. I'm almost frozen."

"What'll we do, Uncle Joe?" Ricky asked.

"Maybe, with your help, I can scramble up the side," he said doubtfully.

We got him up on his one good foot and Ricky climbed out so he could pull from above

53

while I pushed, but we couldn't get him up the steep side of the hole.

Then I remembered Danny. "Wait," I cried. "We'll get Danny's tether rope and let him pull you up. We looped one end of the rope around Danny and the other around Uncle Joe. "Now," I said, "Ricky can lead Danny and I'll help hold you away from the bank." I braced myself between the bank and Uncle Joe. "All right, Ricky," I called.

With Danny's first step, Uncle Joe moved upward in a shower of snow, small rocks and dirt that the rope had torn loose. Safely out of the pit, he sat in the snow, holding his ankle and looking up at us helplessly. How could we get him to the cabin? I worried.

"I know what we can do," said Ricky. "Remember how Grandfather said the Indians used to make a travois to haul things? We'll cut some pine boughs and tie them together with a piece of Danny's rope and let him pull Uncle Joe."

We cut the boughs and tied them the best we could. When we had finished, the remaining rope was so short that Uncle Joe on the branches was right at Danny's heels. If the mule should kick, Uncle Joe would be in trouble.

But Danny didn't kick. With his head down against the storm, he pulled steadily. We stayed close to the creek to keep from getting lost.

Back at the cabin, we got Uncle Joe into his bunk and rolled up his trouser leg to look at his ankle. It was twice as big as it should have been and was awful black looking. But after we'd bathed it in cold water, Uncle Joe said it felt better.

It snowed all the next day and we didn't go out except for wood and water. Uncle Joe's ankle was still badly swollen, but what worried him most was the gold finder. He'd lost it the night before. He kept fretting about it all day and declared he wouldn't go home without it.

Toward the end of the week, the storm cleared suddenly and Ricky and I set off down the creek to the old bear pit. We were scraping around in the snow when Ricky cried, "I've found it."

It was lying on top of a black rock with yellow streaks and shiny specks in it. When we picked up the gold finder, the rock clung to the prongs.

"It's gold!" I cried. "Uncle Joe's gold finder really did find some gold."

We raced for the cabin. Uncle Joe was as excited as we were. He had us pack the wagon, and with a stick for a cane, he got aboard and we set out for home.

We stopped at Uncle Aaron's deserted farm that night and reached Owens' place the next. Owens knew about metals and Uncle Joe could hardly wait to show him the rock. Before we drove in, he cautioned us not to tell where we'd found it. "We don't want to start a gold rush to the place," he said importantly.

He kept right on feeling important too until Owens looked at the rock and started laughing. "It's gold, all right, Joe," he chuckled; "fool's gold! There's iron in the rock and your finder's only a magnet." He touched the prongs to some nails he had in a box to prove it. They clung to the gold finder just as the rock had done.

Well, that just took the wind out of Uncle Joe Bascomb's sails. But he made us promise not to tell what Owens had said. "I'm going to sell that nugget to Sam Snyder," he declared. "I'm going to get my two dollars back. Then he can have his gold finder."

When Uncle Joe came in that evening stamping the snow from his boots, we knew Sam Snyder had bought the nugget. For Uncle Joe had two bright silver dollars and he was looking mighty pleased with himself. He stood in front of the blazing logs, rubbing his hands together, and his gold tooth shone in the firelight, like it was happy too.

4. GHOST HOUSE

Snowflakes were already slapping the windows
of the little red school house when the teacher
tapped the bell that told us it was four o'clock
and we could go home. By the time Ricky and
I had donned our overcoats, caps and mittens
and rushed out with the others, the snow was
coming down in big goose-feathery rolls, frost-
ing the trees and the school house roof and the
crooked rail fence that ran along the highway.

Usually, we followed the fence home, but
today we climbed over it and started across the
woods to our Uncle Ely's house. It was Friday

evening and we were going to spend the week end with Uncle Ely and Aunt Ellen, while Mother and Father were over on the other side of the county visiting Aunt Jane.

Uncle Ely lived about three miles from the school house, but that wasn't much of a walk for us in those days, when roads were few in the Hawpatch and much of the traveling was done on foot or on horseback.

We hurried along, swinging our lunch pails, with the snow stinging our faces and piling up underfoot. We liked going to Uncle Ely's. He told us stories of the early days when buffalo, bears, and wildcats were thick around the Hawpatch. And sometimes he told us about the old ghost house that stood in a clearing a mile or so away. Nobody had lived there for years and years, and Uncle Ely said the place was haunted.

I was dividing my thoughts between the haunted house and Aunt Ellen's biscuits, and wondering if we'd have some for supper, when Ricky stopped suddenly, grabbing my arm and making me stop too. "Chub!" he cried excitedly, "Look! There's a pond! I don't remember ever seeing that before."

We had been through the woods to Uncle Ely's several times, and I'd never seen any pond before either. But, there it was, all frozen over, except for a dark place in the middle.

I hadn't noticed the cold before, but all at once it gripped me, and I shivered all the way down to my toes. "We—we—we're lost!" I gasped.

Ricky's eyes were filled with panic. "What can we do, Chub?" he quavered. "We can't stay out long or we'll free-e-ze."

I could hear his teeth chattering, and mine were clicking too. "Let's keep walking," I said. "We'll come to a house before long."

But I wasn't at all sure that we would. Houses were widely scattered in the Hawpatch, and off the highway, about all we could hope to find would be some trapper's cabin. And even that chance seemed unlikely.

We plodded on, anxiously watching for some familiar landmark; the old hollow sycamore tree where we'd once startled a ground-hog; the fallen log we always walked across, pretending it was a bridge; the string wire fence that marked the beginning of Uncle Ely's farm. But none of them were there.

The snow was coming down faster now and it was beginning to get dark. We were hopelessly lost. It wouldn't do to keep going. We could wander in the timberland for days. I stopped. "Ricky," I said, trying not to sound scared, "we've got to do something."

"But what can we do, Chub?" My brother began to cry. "We're lost," he sobbed, "and nobody'll ever find us."

"They will too," I declared stoutly, although I didn't see how they could. Nobody knew we were lost. Uncle Ely didn't know we were coming, so he wouldn't look for us, and our folks were away and, of course, thought we were at Uncle Ely's. If we were to get out of the woods alive, we'd have to do it alone.

I went through my pockets for matches and found three. Ricky stopped crying. "I've got

61

some too," he said. "Let's build a fire and make us a shelter of branches like trappers do when they're caught out in a storm."

We started gathering brush and heaping it against a tree, leaving a space underneath for us to crawl in. "We'll build a fire right outside," I said. "That'll keep us warm until morning, and then we'll find our way out." I tried to sound confident, but I didn't feel that way. If the sun came out, we'd know which way to go, but it was likely to be cloudy and snowing for several days.

I was scraping the snow out of our shelter when Ricky shouted: "Chub, there's a house!"

I dashed through the woods to where my brother stood pointing through an opening in the trees. Sure enough, there stood a big old two-story house in a clearing. It looked like a very old house and, even from where we stood, we could see that nobody was living in it. Window panes were broken and no smoke rose from the chimney.

Ricky was staring at it like he wanted to run away. "It's—it's the old ghost house," he said, shivering. "I—I—don—don't want to go in there."

"We've got to," I told him. "It's better than being out in the storm."

We stumbled along through the snow toward the house and all the way, something scared and wavery inside me kept whispering, "Ghost house! Ghost house!" The closer we got, the less I wanted to go through that heavy old oak door.

The latch string was out. We pulled it and went inside. The huge empty room echoed our voices and sent tingles of fear slithering down our spines. In the gathering dusk, it looked horribly spooky and I almost wished we had stayed in the shelter we had built.

"We'll kindle a fire," Ricky said matter-of-factly, though he sounded scared.

Outside, we found the deserted wood pile with plenty of half-rotten wood. We carried a lot of it inside, found a bit of kindling and soon had a fire going in the fireplace. Then we sat down to thaw out our half-frozen feet.

Night came down like a buffalo robe

dropped suddenly from the sky. We slipped the bar across the door and pulled in the latch string. We didn't want any ghost walking in on us. There were two other doors leading from the room we were in and a dark gloomy stairway going up into the blackness of the second floor. We locked the two doors with the rusty keys still in the locks, but there wasn't anything we could do about the staircase.

"I'd like to know what's up there," Ricky said fearfully.

"Aw, there's nothing up there," I blustered, "only empty rooms." But the very thought of those empty rooms made me shiver.

We opened our lunch pails. An apple and half a sandwich would have to do us for supper. "I'm hungry," Ricky complained.

"So'm I," I said. "But, anyway, we're getting warm and we won't starve before morning."

With the flames lighting up the room and chasing the black shadows clear to the top of the stairway, we felt a little braver. We sat there warming ourselves and pretty soon we were so sleepy we could scarcely keep our eyes open.

"You go to sleep," I told Ricky. "I'll keep the fire going."

"We'll take turns watching," Ricky said. "You call me in a little while."

Lying on the floor, with his cap for a pillow, my brother was soon fast asleep. I sat facing the stairway and remembering what Uncle Ely had told us. It didn't make me feel any better.

Outside, the wind was rising and snow was coming in through broken windows and sifting in under the door. The old house creaked and groaned and rattled with the violence of the storm. But nothing happened to frighten me, and after awhile, I caught myself dozing. I got up. "There's nothing to be afraid of," I argued. "I'll put some more wood on the fire and take a nap. No use waking Ricky." I put an extra log on the fire and was just stretching out beside Ricky when, all at once, I heard a tapping at one of the windows. I listened. There it was again! Tap! Tap! Tap!" and then silence.

"It's just a branch hitting the glass," I thought. And then, I remembered that there wasn't any tree near the front. Goose pimples popped out inside my stomach. I woke Ricky. "Somebody's tapping on the window," I chattered.

My brother sat up quickly. "Clubs!" he whispered hoarsely, "Clubs!"

We each grabbed a piece of firewood. The tapping stopped as we reached the window. "Maybe it's a ghost," Ricky faltered.

"There aren't any ghosts," I declared. "Father says there aren't."

But Ricky was not convinced, and I wasn't too sure, myself. "Uncle Ely says there are," he countered. Then, "Hear it?" He clung to me, shaking. "It's at the other window."

I stared. A face—an ugly face—was pressed against the glass, peering in at us. It was black and hairy and the eyes gleamed in the firelight. In an instant, it was gone.

My heart stuck in my throat. My legs wobbled. Ricky was white as a sheet and quaking

66

like an aspen. "It—it—it IS a ghost," he choked—"a black one!"

We stood there trembling, clutching each other and the sticks of firewood, and staring at the window. Suddenly, beneath us there was a terrible clatter. Every now and then something would hit the under side of the floor with a loud thump. Our eyes popped as a small section of flooring lifted a little and then fell back into place.

"It's a trap door," I cried. "We've got to hold it down."

Quickly, we piled our stove wood over it, but whatever it was down there, we felt sure could easily lift the wood. The horrible sounds continued in the cellar. We were so scared, the sweat ran down our faces, while inside we were shaking with a chill.

"What'll we do, Chub?" Ricky's voice was a quivery whisper.

All at once, I came to a decision. "Ricky," I said shakily, "we've got to find out what's down there."

My brother clung to me. "No—oo," he pleaded. "We'll be killed."

"We've got to," I insisted. "We can't just stay here like this. We'll take a brand from the fire and our clubs and go look in the cellar."

Ricky stopped whimpering. His shoulders squared. "All—all—right," he said through chattering teeth. I thrust a stick into the flames until one end caught fire, then held it like a torch. "Come on," I whispered.

Quaking with fright, we lifted the bar on the door and went outside, glancing fearfully at the windows. Nothing was there. Cautiously, we moved around the house to the side. The cellar door was open. We could see steps going down into the darkness. All was quiet as we started down, the light from our torch throwing weird shadows around us.

We were halfway down the short stairway, peering ahead, our clubs raised, when, suddenly, we were catapulted into the blackness below. We landed in a litter of rubbish and old tin cans. Luckily, we were unhurt and the torch did not go out. We scrambled to our feet.

There at the foot of the steps stood an old black billy goat. He seemed to be grinning at us.

"It's—it's just an old goat!" I gasped.

And Ricky echoed: "Just an old goat!"

No wonder he had made such a clatter, with all the tin cans in the cellar! And every time he raised his head, his horns would hit the low roof. He had come to the window, attracted by our light and, of course, his horns tapped the glass when he got too close.

I thrust the firebrand at the goat, and he whirled about, leaped up the steps and disappeared in the woods.

We didn't see the funny side of our adventure until we were back by the fire and the excitement had died out of us. Ricky was the first to say what I was thinking. "Let's don't tell anyone an old goat scared us half to death," he said sheepishly. "We'll just say we spent the night in the old ghost house."

"I think a better name would be the old goat house," I laughed.

We heaped wood on the fire and went to sleep. We woke up next morning cold and stiff, to find the sun shining. We knew the house was a mile north of Uncle Ely's and it wasn't long before we were in Aunt Ellen's kitchen, eating hot cakes and maple syrup and bragging about our night in the old ghost house.

"It isn't haunted, Uncle Ely," we said bravely. "We didn't see a thing but one old goat."

5. THE BAYOU TRAIL

The trail along the bayou was muddy and our bare feet sank in the slippery ooze as Ricky and I picked our way through the brush edging the stagnant water. The smell of rotting vegetation hung heavy in the heat of the midsummer afternoon, and the sawing wings of a locust and the lonely call of a dove were the only sounds we heard. Sweat ran down our faces and our shirts stuck to our backs, but neither of us minded too much.

Father had sent us to look for Daisy, our youngest heifer. Daisy had broken out of the cowlot and wandered away that morning and

71

we'd been searching for her ever since. In the afternoon, we came upon a narrow path edging the "new ground" that bordered the timberland along the river.

"Let's follow the path," I suggested.

"Let's," Ricky agreed. "I'd like to know where it goes. Maybe it will lead us to Daisy."

The trail followed a zigzagging path through the timber to the river bank, where it turned upstream, getting wider and muddier as it went.

"No cow ever made that trail," I declared. "It must have been made by a lot of animals over a long time."

"What kind of animals, do you suppose?" Ricky asked.

We stopped to examine some tracks in the mud. They were deep and appeared to be the prints of small sharp hooves, but there were so many of them, we couldn't single out any one clearly.

"Do you suppose they're wild hog tracks?" Ricky's blue eyes held a hint of alarm.

I was wondering the same thing, and I was

feeling uneasy too, but I didn't want to frighten my brother. "Maybe they are," I said, as if it didn't matter. "Anyway, the hogs won't bother us. We'll find Daisy, if she's down here, and be out of the bottoms by sundown."

And then, we had come to the bayou and the wide muddy path had squeezed itself into a narrow boggy strip along the water's edge, with the heavy thicket of vines and roots and brush trying to push it over the brink.

Ricky tossed a rock into the slimy water. It fell with a dull, heavy thud, leaving a hole in the layer of green mould on the surface. "Ugh!" he exclaimed, "I'll bet that water's a mile deep."

"It's not either," I scoffed, "but I'd hate to fall into that old black bayou."

"I won't," declared Ricky.

We followed the path around the bank to a spot where a huge old sycamore spread its branches far out over the water. Here, the trail ended in a small clearing, with thicket all around. In many places, the brush was so dense that no one could go through it without hacking his way. All along, there were round openings underneath, where the hogs had tunneled through. We peered through the thicket and where it was thin enough, we scrambled through it in our search for Daisy.

We found her caught in a tangle of wild grape vines. She kept trying to back out, but the harder she pulled, the more tightly the vines gripped her. With the help of our jack-knives, we finally had the vines cut away and the cow freed. Leading her by the long rope we had brought with us, we started back. By the time we again reached the footpath, the sun was getting low in the west and already the woods was darkening under its umbrella of oak, beech, walnut, and sycamore branches.

We were right under the big sycamore when Ricky pointed to an old abandoned rowboat, rotting in the bayou, a dozen yards or so ahead, and close in shore. We hadn't noticed it as we came in. "Somebody's lost his rowboat," he said.

"It must have been a long time ago," I declared. "It's stuck in the slime, and it looks awful old."

We stood there for a moment, looking at the old hulk and the long, dark shadows sweeping the surface of the bayou, and suddenly I had the strangest feeling that something was going to happen. "Come on, Ricky," I urged. "Let's hurry."

"You scared?" Ricky taunted.

"Of course not," I said. But Ricky must have known that I was, for he turned quickly and started up the path.

Right then, I glimpsed a pair of little red eyes peering from the shadow of a thicket. "Look, Ricky, there's a baby pig," I cried. "Let's take it home."

The pig seemed willing, for it came on out into the open, and I scooped it up in my arms without any trouble. But then, it started squealing and wriggling, so I quickly let it go.

All at once, there was the sound of rushing bodies through the brush, mingled with angry grunts, and suddenly there were little red eyes

everywhere glaring at us in the early dusk.
And these were not the eyes of little pigs, but
of full grown hogs, tall, skinny creatures, with
long legs and wicked tusks sticking out from
their snouts. One old sow came charging down
on us, while the others formed a closed circle
with us in the middle.

Ricky grabbed an overhead branch, screaming at me, and swung himself up out of reach
of the sow. I was only an eyelash behind him.
Somehow, he'd managed to keep his hold on
Daisy's rope. He tied the end of it to a branch.
The sow stopped directly under our perch,
snorting and grunting angrily, but she paid no
attention to the cow.

"Now, what'll we do?" I wailed.

Ricky started to cry, and for once, I didn't
try to stop him. With that old black bayou
behind us and the milling mad brutes down
below, snorting and grunting and wanting to
get at us, there just wasn't any way out. We'd
be stuck there until Father or Jake or somebody else found us, and there was no telling
when that would be. We huddled together in

the tree, trying to think of some means of escape, while night dropped down on us like a bucket of ink. We'd been in a lot of tight places before, but never in one like this.

Suddenly, my brother clutched my arm. "The hogs haven't bothered Daisy," he quavered. "Maybe we could get out riding on her back."

"She'd throw us," I said, "even if they let us get started."

We sat there listening to the angry grunts beneath us and the loud croaking of frogs, and after awhile, a sickly, white-faced moon came out and shimmered a little of its light down through the branches, so that we could dimly see what was going on below. The old sow still paced back and forth under the tree, but we couldn't see any of the others. And then, an idea popped into my head.

"If we could only get to that boat!" I groaned, "maybe we could get across the bayou."

"It hasn't any oars," Ricky objected. "And, besides, we can't leave Daisy."

77

"Maybe we could lead her along the bank, while we kept out from shore just far enough to be out of reach of the sow," I countered. "We've got a long rope on Daisy."

"We could use branches for oars," Ricky put in. "But how can we get to the boat?"

"Ricky," I said, "you know how hogs like to be scratched. Let's get a branch and you try to scratch her back while I go for the boat."

"No, Chub! No!" My brother clung to me, pleading. "It's too risky."

"But we've got to do something," I argued. "We've just got to."

I fished my knife from my pocket and started cutting off a long branch, about an inch thick at the base. Ricky let himself down to the lowest crotch of the tree. When the sow passed close to the trunk, he stroked her back gently with the branch. She seemed not to notice. But, in a few moments, she came within reach again and, this time, Ricky started sawing the stick across her back. She stopped, seeming to like it, and presently she lay down with a satisfied grunt to enjoy the scratching.

78

I crawled out on a low-hanging limb on the opposite side of the tree, to the very edge of the bayou and dropped into the soft mud without making a sound. My heart was chugging like it was pulling a freight train, I was so scared. Peering about me in the darkness for the little red eyes; expecting every moment to hear the rushing bodies and feel the sharp tusks ripping my legs, I hurried toward the spot where we had seen the boat.

At first, I couldn't find it, and my heart did a flop-over and stopped beating. Then, I saw the old hulk a little farther on. The water here was only a few inches below the bank. I stood looking down at it, my skin creeping. What if the floor of the old boat should give way as I stepped into it? I'd go straight to the bottom of the bayou. But then I thought of Ricky scratching away on the hog's back, and I knew I had to go ahead.

Grasping the bow of the boat, I gingerly stepped in and sat down on the cross seat in the middle. By gripping the over-hanging vines and outcropping roots along the bank, I was able to move the boat slowly until a low branch of the sycamore was directly overhead. I swung myself up on the limb and climbed back to Ricky. He was still sawing away with his stick.

"Keep it up," I cautioned. "The boat's waiting. I'm going to tie Daisy to the back of the boat."

I untied the heifer and, climbing along through the branches, I led her to the brink of the bayou. I dropped to the ground and had just finished tying the end of her rope to the stern of the boat when Ricky gave a sharp little cry. I grabbed the limb above me, and my legs wrapped around it in a panic of fear for Ricky. "What is it?" I cried.

Then, I saw. The old hog was getting up, in spite of my brother's frantic efforts to keep her lying down. In a moment, she had ambled out of reach.

"It's all right," I said. "We'll push the boat out from shore with branches. Then, we'll climb way out on a limb and let ourselves into the boat."

We climbed far out on the limb and carefully let ourselves down into the boat.

We cut two leafy branches, pushed the boat out a little, and, with the sow grunting and rooting in the mud beneath us, we climbed far out on the limb and carefully let ourselves down into the boat. The sow's red eyes glared at us across the narrow strip of water between us and the shore. She came down to the very edge of the bayou and, for a moment, I thought she was going to swim out after us. But she didn't.

Using the branches as paddles, we moved the boat slowly, following the bank, and coaxing Daisy by tugging on her rope. The rope tightened, then slackened, as the heifer took a step forward. Suddenly, there was a loud squealing on shore.

"She's stepped on the pig! Look out!" Ricky screamed, but there was nothing that we could do. The sow charged. The next instant, Daisy hit the water with a splash that sent a shower of spume washing over us. The boat whirled, dipped water and almost upset. We clung desperately to the seat, expecting to go to the bottom, but the boat righted itself and Daisy

82

took off across the bayou with the old rotten hulk, stern forward, trailing behind.

Huddled in the bottom of the boat, we clutched one another and held on. I was never so scared in my life, and I could hear Ricky's teeth chattering even above the clicking of my own. The boat was half full of water. We tried bailing it out with our hands, but we didn't make much headway.

We were about halfway across when Daisy began to slow down.

"We'll never make it," Ricky cried, and I could see that we wouldn't.

Maybe Daisy had the same idea, for suddenly she changed her course and headed for the left shore, some twenty yards away. She scrambled up the bank and stood there dripping and bawling, while we clambered out of the boat and untied our tow line. A quarter of a mile farther on, we left the bayou to cut across the timberland for home.

Pretty soon, we saw a lantern bobbing in the darkness and heard Father calling us. We answered and the lantern started toward us.

Ricky nudged me. "Let's not tell about our being scared," he suggested.

Father and Jake came up then, so I just squeezed my brother's arm to let him know I agreed.

"Where did you find Daisy?" Father asked.

"She was in the brush back of the bayou. She was all tangled up in there and we had to chop her out," Ricky said carelessly, as if chopping cows out of the brush were an everyday occurrence.

In the lantern light, I saw his shoulders heave back, and, when he spoke again, there was a strut in his voice. "We'd have been home sooner," he explained pompously, "if we hadn't run into a bunch of wild hogs. One old sow put up a fight."

Father sounded scared. "What did you do?" he asked.

"Oh, we just scratched her back a little," Ricky said, as if it were nothing at all.

84

6. HOME TO ROOST

Ricky and I watched the buckboard, with its cloud of dust, fade into the August twilight, taking Father and Mother to town for an overnight visit with Uncle Zeb's family. We could still hear old Danny's hooves clopping the gravel and the crunch of the wagon wheels when we went inside to light the oil lamp and wash the supper dishes Mother had left for us to do.

Usually, we went along on these trips into town, but lately, the neighborhood had been having trouble with chicken thieves, and we had a fine flock of young hens we couldn't afford to risk losing. So, Father suggested that Ricky and I stay at home. Mother protested that we couldn't stop anyone from stealing the chickens, but Father just chuckled and said he wasn't so sure we couldn't.

We were just finishing the dishes when somebody knocked on the kitchen door, and when my brother opened it, there stood a man we'd never seen before. He was a big hulking fellow, dressed in rough clothes, with an old straw hat pulled down over his face, so we couldn't see him plainly. "Is your pa at home?" he asked in a hoarse, surly voice.

Before he thought, Ricky said: "No, he and Mother are at Uncle Zeb's, and they won't be back until tomorrow morning."

"What did you want with Father?" I asked. "You don't live around here, do you?"

The man mumbled something about buying some hay for his horse, and hastily backed away. We shut the door and something made me lock it and shut and fasten the windows too, although the night was hot. I didn't say anything to Ricky about the way I felt, but I

86

noticed he looked uneasy. "Maybe I shouldn't have told that man Father wasn't home," he said regretfully.

We sat around for awhile, feeling lonesome and just a little nervous, with Father and Mother gone, and no neighbors within half a mile. An old katydid in the woodbox kept chirping and he sounded lonesome too. We listened for sounds outside, wondering if the man who had come to the door was still prowling around. But all we heard was the shrill barking of a dog somewhere and the far-off whoo—oo—whoo—oo of a train speeding through the night. It sounded even more lonesome than the katydid or the frogs croaking down by the pond.

At nine o'clock, we went upstairs to bed, carrying the oil lamp from the kitchen. Nothing had happened to alarm us and we were getting over our uneasiness. The man had gone away and it wasn't likely that he would return. He might have been just driving through and wanting some feed for his horse. With sighs of relief, we undressed, opened the window, and blew out the light. It didn't take us long to go to sleep.

It must have been a little past midnight when Ricky shook me awake. "Chub! Chub! Wake up!" he quavered excitedly. "Somebody's stealing the chickens."

I sat up sleepily. And then I heard loud squawks coming from the chicken house and the frantic flapping of wings as the birds were dragged from their roost.

"What'll we do?" Ricky whimpered.

I was wide awake by that time. "If only we had a gun," I groaned, "we could scare them. But we haven't a thing." Father had loaned his muzzle-loader to a neighbor the day before.

Ricky started to light the lamp, but I stopped him. "We'd better not let them know we're awake," I argued. I pulled on my trousers. "We'll dress and creep downstairs and out the front door," I said shakily. "We'll try to see who they are and maybe we can think of some way to stop them."

"Maybe we could lock them in the chicken house," Ricky said. But I knew he was just wishing out loud, for there wasn't any lock on the chicken house door.

Goose pimples popped out all over me as we felt our way down the stairs to the front door. I was just about to open it when Ricky gripped my arm. "I heard something out there," he choked. "May—may—maybe we'd be-be-better stay inside."

We stood still, listening, but the only sounds we could hear were those of our own heavy breathing and our hearts bumping our ribs. After awhile, I opened the door with fingers so cold and shaky they could scarcely turn the knob.

Outside, the night was black with the threat of rain and no stars to brighten the sky. We crept around the house, making no noise, until we were at the rear. There, we hid behind the rain water barrel and waited. Our eyes had become accustomed to the darkness now and we could make out two shadowy figures coming out of the chicken house with heavily laden sacks thrown over their shoulders.

We followed them out to the road, keeping

out of sight, and saw them dump the sacks into a spring wagon with a canvas cover hooped over the back end. A horse stood in the shafts with head down. We couldn't see to tell much about the outfit or the men, but Ricky thought one of them was the man who had paid us a visit earlier that evening. "He was awful mean looking," Ricky whispered. "What can we do? Oh, what can we do?" he sobbed.

I didn't know what to do either, but I did know we had to keep still. I put a finger on Ricky's lips. "Sh!" I cautioned. "Don't make any noise."

The men were going back to the chicken house with two empty sacks for another load. They were making no attempt to be quiet. "Best haul we've had so far," one of them said, and the other laughed harshly.

I clutched Ricky's hand. It was cold and sticky as my own. "It—it—it's the same one," I whispered, "the man who came to the door."

The thieves were in the hen house now, causing an uproar among the chickens.

"While they're back there, let's dump the chickens out," Ricky said.

We hurried to the wagon and managed to drag out two sacks of our hens. We hid them in a thicket of elder bushes at the side of the road. "That's two sacks of chickens they won't get," Ricky gloated. "We'll unload them as fast as they put them in."

But I knew we couldn't do that. The men had too much of a start on us. They had already made four or five trips before we came out, and we couldn't possibly unload eight or ten sacks of chickens in the time we'd have.

The next trip the thieves made to the hen house, we unloaded two more sacks, and on their final trip, we got two more. We were at the wagon, dragging at a third, when we heard them coming. There was no time to dart across the road to the bushes. "Duck under the wagon," I croaked, dragging at Ricky. Together, we crouched there under the wagon bed while the men dumped their last load under the canvas.

"Well, I reckon that's all, Joe," one of them said. They climbed to the high seat up front and clucked to the horse. "Gid-dap!" We heard the crack of a whip and suddenly the wagon shot forward, leaving us behind.

We started running and in a moment, as the horse slowed down, we were hanging on to the tailgate and wriggling over it into the wagon bed, where we huddled low among the bags of chickens. It was pitch black under the canvas and we had no fear of being seen.

The wagon rumbled along, the men silent, for what seemed to us to be hours. Finally, the driver made a sudden turn to the right and we were off the highway, bumping over rough ground through a thick woods. The men started talking then, and pretty soon one of them said: "We're almost there," and Ricky and I cautiously let ourselves to the ground. When the wagon stopped, we crouched under it, while the thieves got out and tied the horse to a tree. We could make out the bulk of a cabin close by, looming blacker than the woods around us.

"We'll just leave the chickens in the sacks," the man called Joe said. "We'll catch an hour's sleep and be outside the county before sunrise."

The other laughed an ugly, greedy sort of laugh. "This haul will make us a nice piece of money," he gloated. "I hear they're paying fancy prices for spring chickens in Indianapolis now."

Indianapolis! My heart bogged down. Indianapolis was forty miles away. We'd never get our chickens back if they got that far.

Ricky sniffled as the men clumped to the shack and I knew he was thinking that too. We heard the door squeak open and slam shut and in a moment a light shone through the torn shade at the window. We crept to the building and peered inside.

The room was furnished with a bed, a table and a couple of rickety straight-backed chairs. A lighted lamp stood on the table alongside a battered alarm clock, and leaning against the wall was a shotgun. The occupants were about the roughest, meanest and dirtiest looking men

93

we had ever seen, and we felt sure they wouldn't hesitate to use the shotgun on us, if we were unlucky enough to be caught.

The man called Joe wound the clock and set the alarm. Then they pulled off their trousers, blew out the light and went to bed.

We huddled together outside, quivering and with sweat popping out all over us, not knowing what to do. The window was open and the thieves would awaken at the slightest sound. If only we could get the horse and wagon away from the cabin! But I couldn't see any way to do it. We waited tensely until at last loud snores told us the men were sleeping. We crept back to the wagon.

A bold plan was shaping up in my mind. "Ricky," I whispered, "we're going to steal the horse and wagon and take those chickens home."

"But, how?" my brother asked. "They'll hear us sure."

"The ground is covered with pine needles," I said. "They'll keep down the sound of the wheels and we'll back up real slow."

"If they hear us, they'll shoot," Ricky reminded me, and I felt a chunk of ice slither down my spine.

Carefully, we untied the hitching strap and backed the horse a step. The steel rim of a wheel struck a rock and the outfit bounced and rattled as it went over and settled on the other side. We dropped to the ground and scuttled under the wagon as angry voices came from inside the shack, and a man's head was thrust through the window. "Whoa there!" he yelled. "You got fleas or something that you can't stand still?" He came outside and found the strap untied. "I can't figure how that happened," he grumbled. "I would have sworn I tied him up good."

This time, he tied the horse so short that there was no chance for any backing up. He went inside, and after awhile the two were snoring again.

"What'll we do now?" Ricky asked.

We were getting over our fright somewhat in the excitement of trying to save our hens. "Let's clear away any rocks from behind the

95

wheels and try again," I suggested. We felt along the ground behind the wheels and removed what rocks we found. There would be no bouncing this time.

We untied the strap again and eased the horse back a little without making any noise. Another step! The snoring continued. Slowly, very slowly, inch by inch, we backed the wagon, stopping each time to clear away any rocks from the rear of the wheels. It took us a long time, but finally we were some twenty yards from the shack. We decided then it would be safe to turn the outfit around and head out of the woods.

We had to leave the trail to make the turn, and, bounding over the rougher ground, we made some noise. However, we felt safe because of the distance. We had turned around and were just climbing up on the high seat when suddenly a light came on in the cabin and we knew that the loss of the wagon would be discovered quickly. In making our getaway, we had forgotten that the thieves were only going to catch an hour's sleep. That hour had slipped away; the alarm had gone off and we were still within range of their shotgun.

Quickly we grabbed the reins and the whip and gave the horse a cut across the back. The wagon lurched, bounced and rattled until we were sure the men would hear us. Every minute we expected a blast from their shotgun to rip into our backs. But we reached the open road before angry shouts from the cabin told us our enemies had discovered that their horse and wagon were gone. On foot, we knew they couldn't hope to catch us, even if they knew whom they were trying to catch. But, even with this assurance, we kept the horse running full speed. Our main threat now was the shotgun and soon we felt safe even from that.

It took us a long time to reach home, but we were so gleeful over having outwitted the thieves that it didn't seem long to us. Dawn was breaking as we drove into the barnlot. We unhitched the horse, put him in a stall with plenty of corn and hay in the feed box. Then we unloaded the chickens, letting them out in the barnyard to shake their feathers and squawk before setting to work to gobble up the corn we had scattered for them. The chickens hidden in the elder bushes were soon flapping their wings and pecking away with the others.

We left the old wagon behind the barn where it couldn't be seen from the road. Father would attend to it and the horse when he got home. The horse was crunching his corn with a zest that showed how hungry he was, so we gave him some extra ears. "That's to make up for the whipping we had to give you to make you go," we told him.

We stroked his nose and patted his neck, and the old horse stopped chomping long enough to nicker softly and nuzzle our hands, like he somehow understood what we were saying and forgave us for the crack of the whip across his back and the run he had made through the night.

7. PHANTOM OF THE FLATROCK

Ricky and I were just coming in with the milk pails when we overheard Jake telling Mother about the big crop of blackberries that could be had for the picking, some ten miles up the creek from us. Jake had been up-river hunting and had come upon the berries along the Flatrock, which was a branch of the Hawcreek that ran back of our place. There was an old deserted log cabin right near the creek bank, he said, and a spring about a quarter of a mile farther up.

We put the pails on the kitchen table, forgetting to strain the milk, and just stood there gaping, taking in every word.

Jake hesitated, then he went on: "I don't know that I ought to tell you this; I don't want to scare you. But there's something up in those woods that followed me at night. I saw tracks— big ones—but I never saw hide nor hair of whatever it was that made them, though I heard it plenty of times, thrashing through the brush and making a clanking noise down in the river bed." It never bothered him in the daytime, Jake said, but only after dark.

Mother smiled a wistful little smile and shook her head. "I'm not afraid of phantoms, Jake," she said, "but with the threshers coming and all the hands to cook for, we can't possibly go."

We could see that Mother felt bad about losing out on the berries. My brother and I exchanged excited glances. "Chub and I can go," Ricky cried eagerly.

Mother looked doubtful. "I don't know," she parried. "We'll see what your father says."

When Father came in, Mother told him

about the berries and our wanting to gather them. "Well, why not?" he said. "They can take Jake's flatboat, with provisions for several days, and camp in the cabin." He pooh-poohed Jake's story of the phantom. "It's probably a groundhog," he scoffed.

It was still dark outside when Father called us the next morning. We could smell the bacon frying downstairs and hear Father and Jake talking about the flatboat. We dressed and scurried down to breakfast. Then, while Mother packed a huge basket of food for us to take along, we made rolls of our bedding and saddled them on Danny's back for the trip to the river.

By sunup, we were aboard, with our provisions and buckets for the berries. Father cautioned us about handling the flatboat. Then, he shoved us off into the current and we had to paddle hard to keep from going down stream instead of up. The boat moved with painful slowness against the current, and we didn't reach the cabin until dusk.

It was a gloomy looking old cabin, built

of logs, and standing a few yards from the creek, with the timber crowding against it as if trying to shove it into the river. Most of the windowpanes were gone, but there were wooden shutters hanging crazily on one hinge, and half covering the openings. Looking at it, squatting there in the twilight, made me feel shivery, but I didn't say anything.

We carried our provisions into the cabin. Then, because of the heat, we built a fire outside to cook our supper. We fried ham and eggs and set out a loaf of Mother's fresh-baked bread to eat with the honey she'd sent along in a tightly covered bucket. Afterwards, we carried water from the creek to heat over the fire, and washed the dishes. It was too late to go looking for the spring, so we boiled some of the creek water for drinking. Then, by the light of our kerosene lantern, we made up our beds on the floor.

We lay there in the darkness, listening to the night sounds outside. I was thinking about Jake's phantom and wishing we had closed the shutters, when Ricky echoed my thoughts

"Chub," he whispered, "what if Jake's phantom should come prowling around here to-night?"

"Aw, Jake was just trying to scare Mother," I scoffed. "What he heard was most likely a groundhog like Father said. I'm not afraid of a phantom," I added boastfully. "Let's go to sleep."

Reassured, Ricky turned on his side and pretty soon his deep regular breathing told me he had taken my advice. Then, all of a sudden, I heard a loud shuffling, clanking sound outside the door. I clutched Ricky and shook him awake. Together, we listened. "It's the phantom," I quavered.

"The door's barred," Ricky chattered, "but wha-a-at abou—ou—out the windows?"

Shaking with fright, we got up to peer through the window nearest to the door, but we couldn't see anything. We were standing there shivering, debating what to do, when the noises outside stopped, and after awhile we went back to bed.

After breakfast, next morning, we fitted the

hanging shutters into place and shoved them in tight. Then, we set out with empty pails to gather blackberries along the creek.

In front of the cabin, the berries were plentiful and by noon our buckets were filled. We ate some of the berries and some bread and butter before starting out again.

"Let's go all the way up to the spring and work back down," I suggested.

"Let's," agreed Ricky. Then, "Chub, do you suppose that really was just a groundhog we heard last night? It sounded like something big to me."

"It did to me too," I admitted, "but maybe it was just our imagination."

"But it clanked," Ricky argued, "just like Jake said."

"Anyway, it doesn't come out in the daytime," I assured him, remembering what Jake had said.

We had a drink at the spring and then began looking for berries. But we were disappointed. Somebody had been there before us, and whoever it was had not only taken most of the berries, but had torn the vines and tramp-led them underfoot. Suddenly, Ricky cried: "Chub, look at these tracks!"

I hurried over to where he stood. There, in a muddy spot along the creek were two of the biggest footprints I'd ever seen. They looked like the prints of a man's feet, except for their giant size, and they blurred off into the mud, so we couldn't see how many toes there were.

Ricky glanced around uneasily. "If that's the phantom," he quavered, "I hope we don't meet him."

We started working our way down the creek, but it took us most of the afternoon to fill our pails, and we didn't reach the cabin until after sunset.

"We'd better go back to the spring for fresh water," I said. "Mother told us not to drink the river water unless we just had to."

"We'll have to hurry to get back before dark," Ricky warned. Grabbing a bucket, he set off up the creek bank in a trot.

We scooted along as fast as we could, but by

the time we reached the spring, it was already twilight in the timber. Going back, we had to slow down to keep from spilling the water in our pails, and pretty soon the darkness was crowding us so we couldn't see much of anything except the bushes along the river bank. We hurried along, glancing nervously about, seeing vague forms and shadows through the vines, and shying like young colts when a whippoorwill darted out of the bushes and startled us with its weird cry.

We could hear the water babbling along beside us, like it was talking to itself. It sounded lonesome and it made me lonesome too. The night smells were tangy with the scent of cedar and pine, and we could feel the damp mist rising from the water. I was wishing with all my heart that we were back home with Father and Mother, instead of up here in the woods alone, when, sudddenly, there was a loud splash behind us. Fearfully, we looked back. We couldn't see anything, but we heard something huge and heavy hurtle across the creek and crash through the bushes on the shore.

We didn't wait to figure what it was. We ran, screaming and stumbling along in the darkness, trying to hold on to our buckets, with the water splashing our trousers with every step. Still clutching the buckets, our eyes popping with fright, we reached the cabin, panting and puffing and jabbering all at once.

Inside, we slammed the door, bolted it, and fumbled around for the lantern. With it lighted, we felt a little safer, but we didn't dare to go outside to cook our supper and it was too hot to build a fire in the fireplace. So, after we had calmed down a little, we ate some bread and honey and then sat on our bedding roll in the flickering lantern light and listened with strained ears for further signs of the phantom.

"I wish we were home," Ricky said gloomily.

"But we can't go until we pick all the berries," I objected. "Jake would call us fraidy cats and we'd never hear the last of it."

Ricky nodded. "I know he would," he admitted.

Nothing more happened to frighten us, and we finally went to sleep, to awaken with the sunlight streaming in through a crack in the top of a shutter.

We spent the day picking the bushes down stream, but here too, most of the berries were gone and the vines had been dragged down the bank into the river bed. At noon, we emptied our buckets into larger ones at the cabin and ate our lunch. Then we went back to work until early dusk.

We were tired and hungry. I was thinking how good some flapjacks would taste, and wishing we might build a fire outside to cook some. But I forgot all about eating when we came up the bank to the cabin.

My heart popped into my mouth as I saw that the door was wide open. I knew we'd left it closed. A little cry of fear escaped Ricky. He hesitated a moment, then started running for the door. I was right behind him. Whatever was in the cabin, we meant to tackle it then and there. In our anxiety for the berries we'd picked, we almost forgot to be afraid. Quickly, we lit the lantern and looked around.

"Oh! Oh! Oh!" Ricky wailed, and it was all I could do to keep from crying.

Our provisions were scattered about in utter confusion. The honey bucket lay empty and clean on the floor and the berries we had left in the cabin were gone, the empty pails rolled over on their sides.

"All that work for nothing!" Ricky cried.

"No phantom ever did that," I declared angrily. "No phantom could be that mean."

Ricky choked back a sob. "No use crying over spilled milk," he said philosophically, and started looking to see what we could salvage.

The sack of flour had been torn and some of it had spilled, but there was enough left for pancakes, and the marauder had missed the bacon and eggs in the cupboard.

We were busy cleaning up the floor, when I glanced up to see a huge, shaggy form in the doorway. Blocking our escape, was an enormous black bear, standing on his hind legs and staring at us with his little beady eyes.

We shrank back against the opposite wall,

clinging together, our eyes popping with fright. My mind was spinning in circles, trying to think of some way to get out. The shutters on the windows were wedged in so tightly, I knew we couldn't open them. We couldn't climb up anywhere out of the bear's reach. We were trapped!

The huge beast started toward us, walking on his hind legs. We both screamed. The bear hesitated. Suddenly, I remembered something I'd heard Grandfather say about bears. "Be—be-bears do-o-on't li-i—ike noi-oi-oise," I stuttered.

I grabbed the dishpan and started pounding it with a heavy spoon. Ricky snatched up a bucket and started pounding too. But the bear didn't retreat. Instead, he lumbered to the middle of the room and began shuffling around in a circle, forepaws upraised, as if he were dancing with someone. Then, I saw the collar around his neck and the heavy chain hanging down in front, which was almost hidden by his shaggy coat.

"He's tame! Ricky, he's tame!" I cried. "He

belongs to somebody. He won't hurt us."

Gingerly, we approached our visitor. He just stood there, all shaggy and friendly looking, taking us in. At last, we mustered up courage to take hold of the chain. We were over most of our fright now and I could see a new kind of excitement in Ricky's face. "Chub," he exulted, "we've caught the phantom. Let's take him home."

Gleefully, I agreed. We chained old Bruin to a tree and cooked our supper over a fire outside the cabin, and the next morning, we set out for home. We took turns drifting downstream in the flatboat while the other led the bear along the bank.

I never saw Father look so flabbergasted as he did when he saw us leading a bear to the house. "Here's Jake's phantom," we cried. "We caught him."

We told Father about losing the berries, but we didn't tell him how the bear had frightened us. We were still talking excitedly, when we saw a little dark-skinned man, dressed in a red shirt and baggy trousers, coming up the lane.

"You finda my Annie," he cried. "She runa away, breaka the chain."

Annie raised herself on her hind legs. The little man caressed her, scolding her affectionately. "You runa away from Tony. Now, you show boys how you dance." He pulled a French harp from his pocket and played a lively tune. With the bear's paw on his shoulder and his arm around the bear, he whirled around in rhythm to the music, with Annie taking lumbering steps around and around with him. It was funny and we laughed till our sides shook. Then Tony had the bear shake hands with each of us before he set off down the highway with Annie tagging behind.

Ricky's gaze followed the bear wistfully. "I wish we could have kept her," he lamented.

Father didn't say anything. He just stood there with his eyes sort of misty looking and his lips moving ever so slightly, and we knew he was telling God how thankful he was that the bear had eaten the berries instead of my brother and me.

8. THE STORM

My brother and I stood forlornly on the wooden platform and watched the train chug slowly away from the little Hawpatch station, its engine up front belching smoke and its big bell clanging "Ding Dong!" so folks would get out of the way. Mother and Father waved to us from one of the windows. Then the wheels started going clicketty click as they picked up speed. The train got smaller and smaller until it was just a speck down the track and the mournful Whoo-oo-oo-oo—of the whistle floated back to us like it was saying goodbye forever. It was the lonesomest sound in the world.

This was the first time in our lives that Mother and Father had left us to go so far away they had to take the steam cars. They were going to visit Aunt Sarah and Uncle Aaron, who had moved to Missouri. They would be gone a week.

The way I felt about their going was so mixed up it didn't quite make sense. I was proud that Father felt he could trust us to take care of the place so long, and I knew Ricky was too. I could tell by the way he threw back his shoulders as he promised to look after things. But the thought of a whole week alone on the farm made me feel creepy inside.

Father cautioned us about keeping the house locked up when we were away, reminding us that the crop money was stored in an old broken teapot high up on a shelf inside of our kitchen cupboard. The wheat crop had turned out well, so there were several hundred dollars in the teapot. Aside from the butter and egg money, it was all we'd have to take us through the winter until Father sold some hogs or a calf or maybe some of the chickens. He could have put the money in the First National Bank of the Hawpatch, but most of the farmers didn't bother with banks, and Father was one of them.

Mother was worried about leaving us alone, but Father slapped us both on the back and told her she needn't fret; that he'd rather have us in charge than any man he knew. "And, anyway," he added, "Jake will most likely be back before the week is up." Jake had gone to visit his folks down in Kentucky.

It was easy enough to be brave with Father and Mother there beside us, praising us, but now, with them gone and with that old train whoo-ooing goodbye to us, I felt a big lump come up in my throat that choked me and wouldn't come out. Ricky must have felt the same way, for all at once he walked over to a bag of oats on the platform and kicked it as hard as he could.

Dejectedly, we scuffed across the dusty street to the Court House rail, where Fannie Bell and the buckboard were waiting. Neither of us said much on the way home. It was late afternoon when we drove into the barnlot.

We threw down fodder from the mow for the horses, put corn in the feed boxes, and gave some to the cows to keep them quiet while we milked them, and when the outside chores were finished, we went back to the big empty house and fixed our supper. Mother had baked a batch of bread and the fat brown loaves were spread out on the kitchen table to cool. They smelled good. We fried some ham and eggs, and that, with the fresh bread and sorghum, made our supper.

There was something about the empty house that made me uneasy. What if something should happen while our folks were away? I kept telling myself that nothing was going to happen, but that didn't help very much. I was so homesick for Father and Mother, I wanted to cry, and Ricky looked ready to start whimpering too, but he didn't. We just sat around in the August dusk without lighting the kerosene lamp.

At nine o'clock, we were getting ready for bed when Ricky echoed my feelings out loud. "I feel like something's going to happen while Mother and Father are gone," he said gloomily. "I wish Jake would come back."

I'd been wishing the same thing, but I didn't let on. "Nothing's going to happen," I declared stoutly, though I wasn't at all sure that it wouldn't. I got into bed and Ricky followed a moment later.

The old house gave forth with all kinds of squeaks and noises we'd never noticed before. They kept us both on edge. "What's that?" Ricky would ask, nudging me.

"Aw, go to sleep," I'd tell him, "it's only the wind." But then, I'd lie there tense and waiting for the next sound and when it came, I'd nudge Ricky. "Hear it?" I'd whisper.

The last thing I remember before I went to sleep was hearing the clock downstairs bonging midnight. Then, suddenly, Ricky was shaking me awake. "Chub!" he cried, "There's a big storm coming. The wind's blowing a gale."

117

Hastily, we pulled on our trousers and closed the upstairs shutters, then ran downstairs to close and lock the heavy wooden shutters on the ground floor windows. The storm gritted its teeth and came at us in a frenzy. The wind tore at the house, slamming the rain in our faces as we struggled with the shutters against the storm. Lightning crackled about us. Thunder boomed like cannon in the sky. The house shivered, and a brick from the top of the chimney hurtled to the ground. It was the worst storm I'd ever seen.

We were huddled in the kitchen, with the kerosene lamp flickering like it wanted to go out, and casting a sickly glow about the room, when, all at once, there came a loud pounding at the door.

"Jake's home!" Ricky shouted. Before I could stop him, he raced to the door and threw it wide open.

But the burly figure standing outside was not our hired hand, but the ugliest, meanest looking tramp I had ever seen. Long sandy hair straggled beneath his tattered hat, and coarse,

But the burly figure was the ugliest, meanest looking tramp. . . .

red whiskers bristled all over his face like the quilles of a porcupine. Ricky tried to shut the door, but the tramp brushed past him into the kitchen. He carried a heavy cane with a crook handle, and slung over his shoulder was a bundle done up in an old red blanket. He clumped to the middle of the room, his little shoe-button eyes peering out from beneath shaggy brows, darting about, taking in everything, while we just stood there shaking, too scared to move.

A look of intense satisfaction spread over the tramp's face. "Your pa and ma aren't home, I take it," he said matter-of-factly. He put down his bundle and pointed his cane at Ricky. "Fix me some victuals," he ordered, "ham and eggs and coffee, and fry some potatoes, too."

Ricky's face was as white as a ghost and he was shaking even more than I was. "Ye— ye— yes Sir," he stammered.

My legs were so wobbly I could scarcely walk, but I started up the fire in the kitchen stove, while Ricky got out the ham and cut off a big thick slice. Our guest settled himself in a chair beside the table, where he could watch us while we worked.

When the meal was ready, he ate greedily, smacking his lips and sluffing his coffee from the saucer, while his whiskers floated on top, like bushes trailing their branches on a pond.

Ricky and I huddled together on the edge of the wood box behind the kitchen stove, still shaking from fright. The storm was raging outside, and every little while, lightning would cut across the room like it was chasing someone it couldn't catch. I was wishing it would catch the tramp when Ricky nudged me and I knew he was wishing it too.

With his stomach full, the tramp began to show an interest in our belongings. He made us go with him upstairs to Father's and Mother's room, where he ransacked the clothes closet, helping himself to Father's next-best suit. Father was wearing his best one. Then, the tramp went through all the dresser drawers, taking some of Father's underwear, shirts and socks. He carried them downstairs and stacked the clothing alongside his bundle.

After that, he started ransacking the kitchen.

Aside from keeping us in sight, he paid us little attention. I guess he knew we were too scared to do anything, even to run away. My heart was going thubdy-dub-dub as the tramp started in on the cupboard. He'd find the crop money sure as anything, if he took the trouble to climb up so he could see on the top shelf. He was going to do it too! Dumbly we watched him take a chair from the table and place it in front of the cupboard. "Don't reckon your pa'd have some money hid up here some place, do ye now?"

He leered at us and I felt the blood freeze in my veins. What could we do? Oh, what could we do? I wondered. Ricky's eyes were wide with fear, but, all at once, there was something else there too. When Ricky's eyes held that kind of a gleam, it meant he had thought of something. I wasn't long in learning what it was.

The tramp leaned his cane against the cupboard and stepped up on the chair. Suddenly, Ricky jerked open the cupboard drawer, grabbed something brown from it, and dashed to the door, tore it open and disappeared into the storm outside.

I didn't know what he had in mind. There wasn't anything in that drawer except old odds and ends we hated to throw away, but I didn't wait to think about it. I grabbed the cane and shot out of the door behind my brother, just as the tramp jumped from the chair in pursuit. Ricky leaped the back fence and made for the orchard. I was right behind him and the tramp was right behind me. I made the fence, but so did the tramp. He was only a few steps behind me and I could see he was going to catch us, unless—

Suddenly, I leaped to one side and, as the tramp lunged by, I caught his ankle in the crook of his cane and threw him flat in a puddle of water. "Ricky!" I screamed. My brother turned, took in the situation and raced back. "Quick!" I cried, "back to the house!"

We tore across the orchard, over the fence, and through the back yard faster than we had ever run before.

Inside the house, with the door bolted, and heavy shutters barred against the storm, we knew we were safe from the tramp. We sat in the kitchen and chattered nervously over our escapade.

"What did you grab out of the drawer?" I asked.

Ricky giggled. "I don't even know," he said, still shivering from fright. "I just grabbed the first thing I came to. I wanted Old Whiskers to think I had the money." He reached into his pocket and pulled out the brown roll. It was a pair of Father's old socks rolled up, that Mother had put in the drawer to give away, probably to a tramp.

We were sitting there wondering what we'd do when morning came, when somebody started pounding on the door. "It's the tramp," cautioned Ricky.

But then, we heard Jake's voice calling to us to open up, and we did.

"What's the idea of you young ones being up at this time of night?" he scolded.

We told him about our adventure and he

took Father's muzzle-loader and went out, looking for the tramp. After awhile, he came back, saying he couldn't find him, and we went up to bed.

We lay there in the darkness, listening to the rain battering the shingles and watching the lightning frolic about the room. Ricky reached for my hand and squeezed it, and I knew he was thinking the same as I was, that this was a friendly storm. For it had made us lock the shutters, and the old cracked teapot was safe on the cupboard shelf.

9. THE SINGING MINE

It was a snowy evening in November when Father came home from town with the letter from Aunt Sarah in Missouri. She wrote that Uncle Aaron was laid up with rheumatism and unable to do any work. She asked Mother and Father to let Ricky and me spend the winter with them, so that we could do the farm chores for Uncle Aaron.

Ricky and I exchanged delighted glances. Going to Aunt Sarah's meant a ride on the steam cars all by ourselves. It meant living in the hill country of Missouri, where any number of exciting things could happen. But, most important of all, it meant a chance for us to see the Singing Mine that Father had told us about after his and Mother's visit the past summer.

The Singing Mine, Father said, was an old abandoned coal mine, a few miles from Uncle Aaron's place. It was called that because some folks declared they had heard singing down in the old mine shaft. Father scoffed at the idea, though he said Uncle Aaron told him that he, himself, had heard the singing. None of the hill people would go near the place, especially after dark, and Father hadn't bothered to go either.

Mother didn't like the idea of letting us leave home, but because of the emergency, she wrote Aunt Sarah that we'd start the following Wednesday, which was only two days away.

Mother packed a shoe box with fried chicken and cookies and jam sandwiches for us to take along, and Father took down the broken teapot from the cupboard and gave each of us a five-dollar bill for emergencies, he said. We had another dollar apiece for spending money. We strutted about in our Sunday suits, feeling rich and important, and just a little bit scared. We'd been on the steam cars only once before, and Mother and Father had been with us then. We'd have to change cars at Indianapolis, and how would we know which one to take? Would they tell us when to get off? And what if there were nobody to meet us when we got to Lennox Junction?

Wednesday afternoon, we were waiting on the station platform when the train came huffing and puffing to a stop, with a sudden hissing of steam to sprinkle the engine. We stood holding our tickets tightly in our hands while some passengers got off. Then Father lifted our shabby valise to the train platform and followed us aboard. He found us a seat near the front, showed us where we could get a drink, patted our shoulders and left us. We saw him outside talking to the conductor and we knew he was telling him to look after us. Mother was crying a little. She waved goodbye as the train pulled out, and then the wheels were going clicketty click over the rails and we were on our way to the Singing Mine—and, of course, to Aunt Sarah's.

For awhile, we stared out of the window, fascinated by the ever-changing landscape. Then, we remembered the fried chicken and fumbled for the shoe box Father had put under the seat. We ate what we wanted and put the box away. Finally, it began to get dark in the car and a man came through and lighted the gas lamps. We couldn't see much outside now, but pretty soon, the whistle started blowing and the big bell on the engine started clanging, so we knew we must be coming into Indianapolis. Nervously, we clutched the valise and the shoe box, and then the conductor came by and said: "All right, boys. Here's where you get off."

He had us wait beside him while he helped the rest of the passengers down. Then, he led the way into a big waiting room, with long benches where people were sitting with their baskets and bundles about them. He left us in charge of an old man in a blue uniform like his own. We waited a long time, it seemed, before the train caller shouted through a big horn: "Trains for Terre Haute, St. Louis, Springfield, and points west." He named a lot of other places besides, but none of them was Lennox Junction, where we were supposed to get off. But we knew our train would go to Springfield, and we started looking anxiously for the old man. Right then, we saw him coming. He led the way to a seat in one of the middle cars, told us we'd be in Lennox Junction late the next afternoon, and went back to the station.

The train pulled out, and pretty soon, the conductor came through and turned the lights down low, so folks could sleep. But Ricky and I were too excited to think of sleeping. We sat staring out into the darkness as the train plunged through the night, and after awhile, a big fat moon came from somewhere and started west with us. I was watching the dreary landscape, with its miles and miles of snow-covered plains, when Ricky poked me. "I wonder what's down in that old mine shaft," he brooded. "Do you suppose it's a ghost or something?"

"Ghosts don't sing," I scoffed, but I was wondering, too, what it could be.

We reached St. Louis the next morning and there was a long wait while our car and some others were unhooked and placed on a siding and another engine backed up and clanked into us to be hooked up. Then, we were off again, and by late afternoon, we were in the hills of southern Missouri. We struggled into our overcoats and arctics, pulled on our caps, and, clutching our half-empty shoe box and our valise, we waited anxiously for our station to be called. "I hope Aunt Sarah's there to meet us," I worried.

"Of course, she'll be there," Ricky asserted, but there was a frightened look about him that told me he wasn't sure.

At last, the conductor came in and announced: "All out for Lennox Junction," and we hurried up the aisle to the rear platform, clinging to the backs of seats, as the train lurched and jerked to a stop. We were the only ones to get off, and it seemed that our feet had scarcely touched the ground when the conductor swung himself aboard and the train was moving on.

We looked around, hoping to see Aunt Sarah, but no one was in sight. We had thought that Lennox Junction would be a town, but there was nothing here except a blacksmith shop, a few ramshackle houses, and a country store, unpainted and leaning to one side. The place looked deserted. We went to the blacksmith shop, but no one was there. The door to the store was padlocked, and bore a big sign: "CLOSED."

"No use trying the houses," I said. Anyone can see they're empty.

"What'll we do, Chub?" Ricky quavered. Panic was in his eyes.

"I don't know," I said. "I guess we'll have to walk to Uncle Aaron's."

"But, which way is Uncle Aaron's?" he wailed.

I didn't know. We were standing there, trying to decide what to do, when we saw a horse and wagon coming toward us. When we asked the driver where Uncle Aaron Abernathy lived, he said the Abernathy farm was some seven miles north of where we were. He was going up that road about three miles and would be glad to have us ride with him that far.

It was after sundown when we clambered out of the wagon and the farmer turned up a side road, after telling us to stay on the main road and we'd come to Uncle Aaron's about four miles farther on.

The road wound up and down and around through the heavily wooded hills. It was hard walking, though the snow was tightly packed. We were warm and snug in our heavy clothes and, now that we knew we were going in the right direction, we weren't too worried until we got to wondering what kind of wild animals the woods might hold. As we scurried along through the gathering dusk, we picked up a couple of heavy sticks to use as weapons, in case a bear or a panther should appear.

Darkness was just swallowing the twilight

when we came to a place where the road branched, one part going north-east, and the other, north-west. One looked about as well-traveled as the other. Both were dirt roads, deeply rutted, and covered with hard-packed snow. We took the one to the right. "It can't be more than two miles more," I said. "I'm sure we've come at least two miles since we left the farmer."

On and on, we trudged, over seemingly endless miles. The road narrowed to a trail. "Oh, Chub," Ricky wailed, "we're on the wrong road. I know it."

I knew it too. We stopped. With a sinking heart, I stood there, crying inside like a baby, but trying not to let on how terribly worried I was. My brother was whimpering. "What can we do? Oh, what can we do?" he sobbed.

I pinched him to make him stop crying. "Don't," I said huskily. "We've got to do something. It's too far to go back to the other road tonight. Let's build a fire and camp here."

Ricky sniffled. "Let's," he agreed wearily.

We began fumbling under the trees that

edged the trail, picking up sticks for a fire. We had a small blaze going, when suddenly Ricky stopped and clutched my arm. "Listen!" he cried. "Do you hear that?"

Faintly, the strains of "My Old Kentucky Home" fluttered on the night wind, ebbing away, then coming in full and clear, to ebb again. "It's a man singing!" Ricky exulted. "He can't be far."

We shouted again and again, hoping that whoever it was would hear us, but the singing continued. We started toward the voice. Back in the woods a short distance, was what looked like a huge pile of brush banked against the side of a hill. "It's coming from there," Ricky said, and started pulling the brush apart.

Then, all at once, it struck me. "Stop! Ricky, stop!" I cried. "It's the Singing Mine!" But I was too late.

Ricky screamed once, a terrified, piercing scream. Then, I was standing alone there in the darkness, the sweat popping out all over me, my heart flat on my stomach. Ricky had fallen into the black mine shaft.

135

The singing had stopped when Ricky screamed. I called to him, but there was no answer. I lit a match, but the light was too dim to make out anything except the gaping black hole before me. I started screaming.

Then, suddenly, the mine shaft was flooded with yellow lamp light, as a door opened below and a man, with a lighted lamp in his hand, stood in the doorway. Ricky lay crumpled at the bottom of a short flight of steps. I flung myself down them and tried to lift him up. "He's hurt," I sobbed. "Maybe he's dead."

The man set the lamp down and examined Ricky. "I don't think he's hurt much," he said reassuringly, "maybe a bad bump on the head."

He pulled off Ricky's cap and there was a big bump coming up on his forehead. My brother opened his eyes. "What happened?" he asked.

I was so relieved, I started bawling just like a baby, and I couldn't stop.

Ricky sat up. "I'm all right," he said.

The man helped him through the door into a large room which evidently served as living quarters. There was a makeshift fireplace built of rocks, a home-made table, a three-legged stool and a bunk against the wall. And, in one corner, on the floor, there was a square wooden box with a big horn on top.

Our host was a young man, fair-skinned, and with hair the color of bright copper. Right away, we liked him. His name was Thadeus Hargrove, he said, and we could call him Thad. He told us he was prospecting in the hills and had holed up in the old mine, after flooring the shaft at the first level. "It's nice and cool down here in summer," he explained, "and warm in winter, too."

We told him all about our trip and what people said about the Singing Mine. He laughed heartily when we said folks were afraid of the mine because of the singing. Then he walked over to the box with the horn on top, turned a little crank, and the strains of "My Old Kentucky Home" started coming through the horn, out of the box. We stared, wide-mouthed. "It's a talking machine," Thad explained, "the first one to reach these parts,

137

I suspect. It gets lonesome out here sometimes, and so I got it to keep me company."

Our new friend put some salve on Ricky's bump and gave us each a big bowl of rabbit stew. Afterwards, he insisted that we sleep in his bunk, while he made a pallet on the floor.

The next morning, Thad gave us pancakes for breakfast. He said he didn't know our Uncle Aaron, but said there were some farms along the main highway. He cut across the woods with us until we came in sight of the main road, but he wouldn't go on with us to Uncle Aaron's.

"I'd rather not," he said, "and if you boys don't mind, I'd just as soon you didn't tell anyone the secret of the mine." He grinned a friendly, chuckling sort of grin. "I really don't care much for company, except for boys like you, who just drop in on me."

We had to laugh at that one. We really had dropped in on him. We promised not to tell anyone about his living in the mine, since that was what he wanted. Then he waved goodbye to us and strode back through the timber.

A half mile or so up the road, we came to a weathered old farm house, with the name, "Aaron Abernathy" painted in big black letters along one side of the barn. We found Uncle Aaron propped up in a chair by the fireplace.

Aunt Sarah cried when she saw us. Uncle Aaron hadn't been well enough for her to leave him to go into town for the mail until the day before, and by the time she'd read Mother's letter, the train had been through Lennox Junction and we had disappeared.

"Where did you spend the night?" she asked, helping us off with our overcoats.

Ricky gave me a look to keep still. "Oh," he said carelessly, "we got off on the wrong road and ran into the Singing Mine, so we spent the night there, down in the old mine shaft."

Aunt Sarah's face paled. I thought she was going to faint.

Uncle Aaron's mouth flew open in amazement. "Di—did you hear the singing?" he asked.

"Oh, yes," Ricky said indifferently, "but it

didn't bother us any. Who's afraid of an old mine shaft!"

"Or a singing ghost!" I added with a shrug.

We gloated over our secret until the next day, when Aunt Sarah brought home a copy of The Farmer's Weekly. There on the front page, was a picture of Thadeus Hargrove, with some printing underneath that said he was wanted by the sheriff for robbing a bank in Springfield.

We had to tell what we knew then, and Aunt Sarah took us into town to tell the sheriff. He sent a posse to the mine, but Thadeus had fled, taking with him the little box with the horn on top and the ghost of the Singing Mine.

10. WILD GOOSE CHASE

Rain lashed the window panes and Ricky and I could hear the branches of the old elm tree outside slapping the shingles as we climbed the stairs to bed, with the flickering oil lamp throwing its feeble beams into the shadows above.

We'd been at Uncle Aaron's only a few days when Aunt Sarah decided to take him to Springfield for treatment by a doctor she'd been hearing about. They would be away all winter.

It was lonesome in the old farmhouse, without any grownups around, and sometimes it was scary too. For Uncle Aaron's farm lay back among the hills, with the nearest neighbor over a mile away. Around the clearing, heavy timber stretched in all directions except for the narrow dirt road that went sneaking out toward the sunset.

This was one of the scary nights. I shivered, not from the cold, but because I was thinking how alone we were, and because I had a feeling that something was going to happen. Then I noticed that my brother was shivering too, even while beads of sweat clung to his forehead. "Chub," he quavered, "wouldn't it be awful if something happened to make us go out in this storm?"

"Aw," I bluffed, "nothing's going to happen. Are you scared?"

Ricky stiffened. "Of course not," he sniffed, "are you?"

I didn't answer. Gloomily we undressed, blew out the light, and went to bed, to lie there listening to the rain battering the rooftop and swishing along the gutters to the rainwater barrel below.

It seemed that I'd been asleep only a few minutes when suddenly I was awake. The clock downstairs struck eleven. Then I heard a faint scratching sound and the plaintive yelping of a dog. I awakened Ricky and we went downstairs. When we opened the door, a small black and white dog shot past us into the room, shaking the rain from his coat.

I took him in my arms, but he broke away and ran to the door, whining and scratching to get out, just as he had done to get in.

"He's begging us to follow him," Ricky said. "Are—are we going to?" He sounded scared, and I felt my skin creep. The thought of going out into the storm in the middle of the night to follow a strange dog through timber we didn't know, started goose pimples popping out all over me. But, scared as I was, I knew we had to go. "Of course, we're going," I declared. "Somebody must be in trouble."

We put on our overcoats, boots and caps and set out, carrying the lantern. With the dog running ahead, we crossed the orchard and the meadow beyond. Then we were in the timber, picking our way through wet underbrush. The rain had stopped, but heavy clouds still swept across the sky. On and on we went, our faces scratched by thorny branches, our mittens soaked in fending off the blows. "Where do you suppose he's taking us?" Ricky grumbled. "We must have come more than a mile."

"Maybe on a wild goose chase," I said, "but we've got to know."

The dog stayed just inside the circle of our lantern light, whining softly, and looking back at us, moving ahead as we moved, coaxing us on.

I could feel little shivers creeping up and down my back as we trudged through the wilderness night, smelling the wild tang of rainwashed pines and hearing the wind soughing through the branches. It sounded lonesome and somehow frightening, like ghosts whispering to one another and sighing because they were sad. Then, all at once, my ears caught another sound; a low moaning, as of someone in pain. My heart almost stopped beating. It might be a panther in the brush. I grabbed

Ricky's arm. "Hear that?" I whispered shakily.

We stood still, listening. It came again, lifted for a moment, then faded into the breath of the night wind. The dog's whine changed to a yelp. He looked at us pleadingly, ran a little ahead and back again, as if to say: "Come on; there's nothing to be afraid of."

"The dog's not afraid," I said. "He would be if a panther were around."

We started forward again. We had gone only a few yards when the dog broke away from the lantern light and dashed ahead of us, barking and yelping. Following the barks, we found ourselves in a small clearing down in a hollow. A log cabin loomed up in the lantern light.

The dog headed straight for the half-open door and we followed him in. The place was dark, but in the glow of our lantern, we saw a man lying in a bunk against the wall. There was no other furniture in the room, but a rude ladder went up the wall to a hole in the ceiling, apparently to a loft. The man in the bunk was tied hand and foot.

"Who tied you up?" we asked.

He groaned. "I don't know," he said weakly. "I stopped here for the night and three men forced their way in. They shot me in the leg when I tried to get to my horse." His name was Wiggins, he said, and the men had robbed him of his money.

With my knife, I started to cut the rope binding his wrists, but he stopped me. "They'll be back," he said. "I can't walk with this bullet in my leg, and if they find me untied, they'll know someone's been here. You boys take my horse and go for help. And blow out that lantern."

"We'll bring help," we promised.

We blew out the light and were about to slip out of the door when suddenly we heard the clatter of hooves down the rocky slope into the hollow, and then the loud voices of men as they dismounted. They were upon us! We couldn't leave through the door! "The ladder!" I croaked.

We scurried across the room and up the ladder, carrying the lantern. We had just cleared the opening into the loft when we

146

heard the heavy clumping of boots on the cabin floor. There was an opening in one of the gable ends of the loft, where once a door had been. Stealthily we crept across the rough boards to the opening. But there was no outside ladder by which we might climb down, and the men would surely hear us if we jumped.

"How are we going to get down?" Ricky asked.

"Sh!" I cautioned. I felt along the outside edge of the opening. There was a hinge still hanging there. I nudged Ricky. "Give me your suspenders," I whispered.

"What for?" he objected. "My pants will fall down."

"I've got to have them for a rope," I said, stripping off my own.

With my knife, I cut the pairs apart and tied the four pieces together. I fastened one end to the hinge and tested it for strength. Ricky went down first with the lantern. Then I started down. I was about halfway when suddenly our make-shift rope snapped and I

147

dropped some five feet to the ground, still clutching part of the suspender rope. Luckily I wasn't hurt, but the men had heard us, for the noise inside stopped instantly. My pants were down. I jerked them up and we ran as fast as we could for the timber. We had just reached cover when we heard the robbers outside, shouting and yelling to one another. We waited breathless.

"What'll we do, Chub? What'll we do now?" Ricky wailed. "I can't keep my pants up," he complained.

I still had two pieces of the suspenders. I gave him half, and we hoisted one side of our trousers.

In a little while, we heard the men go inside and slam the door, evidently satisfied that some animal had made the noise they heard. We skirted the cabin until we were on the other side, where Wiggins had left his horse in a leanto stable. A sickly moon peered down at us through the clouds as we sneaked across the clearing to the shed. The horse was gone.

"We'll have to take one of their horses," Ricky whispered in my ear.

My heart pounded wildly at the thought. If they caught us, they'd hang us for horse thieves. But there didn't seem to be any other way. Quaking in our boots, we crept around to the front. In the faint sprinkling of moonlight, we saw four horses, three of them with saddles. The fourth, a big bay, we figured belonged to Wiggins. We took the bay. We were used to riding bare back, so that didn't bother us any. We could hear the men talking and laughing as we untied the horse and led him away, keeping in the shadows as much as possible.

At the edge of the timber we mounted. Then, I realized that we didn't know which way to go. We had blindly followed the dog to the cabin, without thinking which way we were going, and now we were lost. Lost, while a wounded man in the clutches of thugs waited for us to bring help!

All about us lay the densely timbered hills,

and so far as we could see, no trail led out. We were sitting there, wondering what to do, when one of the men came out of the cabin. Suddenly we heard him shout: "The horse is gone! Somebody's stolen the horse!"

There were more yells and curses as the robbers mounted and went galloping out of the hollow. A bold plan was forming in my mind. "Ricky," I said, "we'll let them show us the way out. They'll think whoever took the horse is ahead of them on the trail. Instead, we'll be behind them. If we hear them coming back, we'll hide in the timber."

The sound of hoofbeats was growing dimmer. "We'll have to hurry or we'll lose them," Ricky worried.

With my brother behind, holding on to me, we set out in pursuit. We soon found ourselves following a rocky trail. I was wondering where it would take us when Ricky poked me. "Chub," he said uneasily, "I don't hear their horses any more. Maybe they're waiting for us."

We stopped and dismounted. Leaving the trail, we crept along in the shadow of the timber, leading the bay. We had gone about a mile, when we again heard the pounding of hooves. "Sh!" Ricky whispered, "they're coming back."

Hidden in the thicket, we waited. They came charging up the trail, cursing their luck and swearing vengeance on the one who had taken the horse. We held our breath as they went past. The sound of their voices was dying away in the distance and we were gloating over our escape, when suddenly the big bay raised his head in a loud and prolonged neigh. My heart thudded down on my stomach.

"He's gone and done it now," Ricky groaned.

The sound of retreating voices stopped abruptly. We knew the men were turning around to come back. They'd find us sure. "We'll have to race them," I choked. "It's our only chance."

Quickly we mounted and headed down the

trail. Kicking the bay in the flank, we got him running, but the robbers were gaining on us. We heard them yelling for us to stop. A bullet zipped past us. "Kick him, Ricky! Kick him harder!" I cried.

Bent low on the horse's neck, with Ricky clinging to me and kicking with all his might, we streaked down the trail faster and faster. It was as if the big bay knew he had blundered us into this scrape and was doing his best to get us out.

The cries of the men grew dimmer, then suddenly they stopped altogether. In a moment, I saw why. We were coming into a little town where they dared not follow. "Ricky," I cried, "we're safe! We beat them! We did! We did!"

There was a light coming from the hotel. We tied the bay and went inside, where a man dozed by the fire. We told him about the robbers and the wounded man and he routed out the sheriff. In a little while, we heard the law men go galloping up the trail. I drew a deep breath and let it out with a whish. "My!" I exclaimed, "I'm glad that wild goose chase is over. Aren't you, Ricky?"

But Ricky didn't answer. Already, he was fast asleep in his chair by the pot-bellied stove.

11. A FRIEND IN NEED

That winter Ricky and I spent at Uncle Aaron's was the worst we had ever known. It started raining in November and didn't stop until mid-December, when the heavy snowfall began. The February thaws brought more rain and by March, the rivers were running bank high. That's how it was the evening old Shep came to us.

We had just finished the chores that evening, when a big shepherd dog came into the barnyard and followed us to the house. We fed him a chunk of ham, with a meaty bone to

chew on. Then, we made him a bed in the cellar and went in to fix our own supper. After-
ward, we sat by the fire, watching the rain spat-
ter the windows, with the wind whipping it to
a froth.

In spite of the fire, I shivered. "No wonder
old Shep wanted to get in somewhere," I said.
"Do you suppose he belongs around here?"

"I hope not," Ricky said eagerly. "I'd like
to keep him."

I nodded. "Me too."

At nine o'clock, we climbed the stairs to
bed. With the rain pounding the shingles and
the elm tree scraping the eaves, we went to
sleep. Then, all of a sudden, I awoke with a
start, to the sound of loud frantic barking. I
nudged Ricky. "Old Shep's barking his head
off," I said. "We'd better see what's the matter
with him."

Ricky sat up shivering. "We'll have to go
outside to get in the cellar," he grumbled.
"We'll get soaked."

"We'll dry out," I told him crossly. I wasn't
anxious to get a soaking either, but I knew

something was wrong with the dog. We had to find out what it was.

We dressed quickly and hurried downstairs. The clock, in its niche over the mantel, bonged midnight. We counted the strokes as we stood hesitating at the kitchen door, dreading to go outside, yet knowing we had to.

The barking continued, more frantic than before. The rain came down in torrents, slamming against the house like it was daring us to open the door. But it wasn't just the rain that held us back. I was thinking that maybe a wolf or a panther or some other wild animal might be outside. Maybe that was why old Shep was barking. "Let's take some clubs along, and the lantern," I suggested.

Ricky's eyes widened with fright. "Let's wait awhile," he pleaded. "Maybe we won't have to go. Maybe Shep will stop barking if we wait."

"No," I said sharply, "we've got to go now. Come on."

We each grabbed a stick from the woodbox and, with the lighted lantern, we opened the door, stepped outside, and stopped in amazement. The house stood in what appeared to be a huge lake. The building, standing on a very high foundation, was well above the water, but it was washing over the slanting cellar doors. When we opened them, we found the cellar almost full of muddy, swirling water.

The frantic dog shot by us in a flying leap, to land on the porch, shaking the water from his shaggy coat. We scrambled up beside him, already drenched to the skin. We were standing there, scared and miserable, and wondering what to do, when a man on horseback dashed up to the porch, yelling that the river had broken through the levee and for everybody to get to higher ground. Then he was gone before we had a chance to say anything.

Our nearest high ground was on some hogback hills that rose from the pasture land, a hundred yards or so back of the barn. For, although Uncle Aaron's farm was in the hill country, the buildings, orchard and barnlot were cupped in the valley between.

Ricky started to whimper. "What'll we do,

Chub? What'll we do? We'll drown if we go out there. Let's stay in the house, upstairs."

I was as scared as my brother, but I wasn't just thinking of us. I was thinking of Uncle Aaron's horses and cows and pigs. He'd trusted us to take care of them. "Ricky," I quavered, "we've got to save Uncle Aaron's livestock. He and Aunt Sarah depend on them for their living."

"But how?" Ricky stood there shaking, his eyes wide with fear.

Icy chills chased each other along my spine, but I managed to keep the quiver out of my voice. "We'll each get on a horse," I said boldly. "We'll put the other six horses on lead ropes and lead them to the high ground. And we'll turn the cows loose and try to drive them. We can't save the pigs and the chickens."

"We can turn the pigs loose," Ricky argued. "Maybe they'll swim to the hills."

We waded out to the stable, saddled two of the horses and lined the others up on lead ropes. Hastily, we let down the rails to the pigpen. The chickens were high on their roosts in the hen house. They'd be safe enough for a while.

Uncle Aaron had eleven cows. We let them out of the barnlot and started driving them toward the nearest hogback. Now, that we were actually fighting to save Uncle Aaron's animals, we didn't have time to be afraid. The water was getting deeper and deeper. It was hard work riding and leading three horses and trying to keep the cows headed toward the hill. The pigs were swimming in all directions and I knew we couldn't do anything with them.

"We'll get the horses and cows to safety and come back for the pigs," Ricky said, but I knew we couldn't do that. We'd be mighty lucky if we got some of the cows to higher ground. Everything seemed to be going smoothly. I was thinking how glad Uncle Aaron would be to learn we'd saved the horses and cattle, and I was beginning to feel good inside again. We were within a hundred feet of the hill, with the cows moving ahead of us, frightened and bawling, when, all of a sudden, one of them broke away from the group.

Ricky turned back to round her up. I yelled to him to keep going. "We'll lose them all if they scatter now," I warned him, but I was too late. Two more cows broke away to follow the first one. Then, suddenly, all of them were lifted by the water, so that their feet no longer touched the ground. Bawling and struggling, they swam in circles. The horses too were swimming now and it was all we could do to keep them headed for the hill. "Come on!" I shouted to Ricky, who was trying desperately to round up the panicked cattle, while his horse and the three on his lead rope floundered in the muddy current. Reluctantly, Ricky obeyed.

We watched Uncle Aaron's cows drift away behind us, and a lump came up in my throat that I couldn't swallow. Uncle Aaron had to have those cows. He just had to. We climbed the slope of the hogback, and tethered the horses, both of us crying inside.

For a moment, we stood there in the darkness, staring out over the black waters of the flood, thinking of Uncle Aaron and Aunt Sarah and what this would do to them. Then, all at once, I had an idea. "Ricky," I cried excitedly, "let's turn the horses loose. They won't go back into the water. We can take their lead ropes and try to round up some of the cows. Maybe we can bring them in like we did the horses."

"But Chub," Ricky objected, "we'll drown."

"No, we won't," I insisted, though I was just as scared of drowning as Ricky. I guess he knew it too, for he didn't say anything more.

We took Ginger and Dido, the two youngest and strongest horses in the lot, but neither of them wanted to go back into the flood. We found a couple of short sticks and with their prodding, we managed to get our mounts into the water again. Some fifty yards from the hogback, we came upon the milling, floundering herd. We managed to get three of them on the lead ropes, and started back, driving the others. The cattle were almost exhausted, but still they kept trying to break away and turn back.

"We'll never make it," I groaned, but I didn't say it out loud. I knew we had to make it. We yelled and prodded until all the cows were within a few yards of the hill, when one of them broke away again and headed back into the flood. Some of the others started to follow. My heart bogged down on my stomach. It was no use. We'd have to let them go. Three of the cows were still ahead of us. We might be able to save them, but the other five, we couldn't.

Ricky started to turn back, but I called to him: "Let them go," I cried. "We can't save them now."

Right then we heard a loud barking, and a huge shaggy form came splashing through the water. It was old Shep. In the excitement, we'd forgotten all about him. He went to work on those cows as if he'd been herding cattle all his life, and soon had them lined up, bawling loud protests, but aiming straight for

162

the hogback. Up the slope, they floundered, with old Shep behind them, nipping the stragglers' heels.

There in the mud, we got down on our knees to hug our staunch ally, the shepherd dog who had helped us save the cows.

We found a tiny cave in the hillside and, after several attempts, we managed to start a fire outside, under a sheltering rock. We huddled there until daybreak, but Shep wouldn't stay with us. When we tried to hold him, he whined and pulled away. We could hear him barking through the rest of the night, somewhere on the hill. "What do you suppose he's up to?" Ricky questioned.

I didn't know and I was too tired to care. I yawned. "Whatever it is, it's all right with me," I declared. "He saved five of the cows for us."

"I wish we could have saved the pigs too," Ricky lamented.

"Me, too," I said. "Losing his pigs is going to be hard on Uncle Aaron, but there's no use crying over spilled milk, I guess." I hunkered down in my wet clothes and tried not to think about the pigs.

In the warmth of the fire, we finally dozed off. Then suddenly we were awake and it was day again. The top of the hill was an island, with the flood waters spread out as far as we could see, and little islands rising here and there where hogbacks had been before. The rain had stopped and the sun was coming up behind us on the other side of the hill.

Old Shep was nowhere around. We called to him and whistled, but he didn't come. The horses and cows were all there, but where was the dog? We started walking toward the other end of the hogback. Topping the ridge, we stopped and stood stock still, unable to believe what we saw. Uncle Aaron's pigs were rooting around in the mud, just as if nothing had happened, and old Shep was stretched out on the ground between them and the water, fast asleep.

Now, we knew why he hadn't come to help us sooner. He'd been rounding up the pigs. Something inside me gave way then and I started crying just like a baby. Ricky was crying too and presently old Shep woke up and came over to lick the tears from our faces. We hugged him to let him know how glad we were and just to say "Thank you." I'm sure he understood us too, for he wagged his tail and barked, and, in dog language, we knew he was saying, "You're welcome."

12. THE SHORTEST WAY HOME

Ricky and I were already late starting for home that evening, when Aunt Hetty called us back to give us a can of red pepper she had been saving for Mother. We had been working for Uncle Ben that week. On this particular evening, there had been extra chores to do, so we had stayed for supper before setting out on the three mile walk home through the timber. That is, it was three miles if we went around by the old covered bridge over Haw Creek. But we could save a mile by using the railroad bridge that straddled the river farther to the north.

Father had warned us not to use the railroad trestle. He said it was too dangerous. That was all right in the daytime, but I didn't like the idea of going through the old covered bridge after dark. It was scary going into that gaping black hole, where you couldn't see your hand before your face, but I wouldn't admit being scared. So, after we'd left Uncle Ben's, I started talking about how tired I was and then I suggested, sort of off-hand, "Let's use the trestle."

"Let's," Ricky agreed so quickly that I knew he'd been thinking about it just the way I had.

The night was as black as a summer night could be, with clouds smudging out all the stars. A misty dampness had crept in with the dusk and we could smell the sharp, sweet breath of the pines and hear the drowsy night noises of the timber.

We hurried along with sticks in our hands to use in case we should meet a bear or a panther or maybe a timber wolf. Some of the farmers had been losing calves and sheep and later coming upon their half-eaten carcasses in the timber, so we were more than a little nervous and very much on guard. Nothing happened to frighten us, however, and before long, we came upon the railroad, going the same way we were until it crossed the river. Then it veered off to the left, while we had to go straight ahead to reach our place.

When we came to the trestle, I almost wished we'd chosen the covered bridge, but I didn't say anything. I knew Ricky was feeling uneasy too. We could hear the swish of the water below us as we picked our way over the rails, and smell the dank, fishy tang of the mist swirling up to lick our faces. We strained our ears for the sound of an approaching train. I was trying to figure out what we would do if one should come along, when suddenly I heard a sharp, grating noise and then the clink of iron striking iron, as if someone were hammering the rails. The sounds came from somewhere ahead of us down the track.

Ricky heard it too. He grabbed my arm.

"What do you suppose it is?" he asked anxiously. "Could it be a train?"

I didn't know what it was, but I knew it wasn't a train. "No," I told him, "no train ever sounded like that."

We crept forward cautiously until we reached the end of the trestle. Then we slipped down the bank and into the edge of the timber that hugged the track on both sides. But, instead of turning off toward home, we followed the track, determined to find out what was making the scraping, clinking sounds we could still hear just ahead. They were much louder now. Some fifty feet from the river, we made out the shadowy forms of two men, busily driving a spike between the rails.

"What are they doing that for?" Ricky whispered. "Sh!" I squeezed his arm for silence. We waited tense and listening. My heart was pounding like mad. What were those men up? I wondered fearfully. We could see them bending and straining and hammering and hear the loud scraping and clinking as they worked.

169

"Looks like they're prying a rail loose," I whispered in Ricky's ear.

"What would they do that for?" Ricky's voice was frantic. "They'll wreck the train!"

"Maybe they want to wreck it," I said. A shiver slid down my back into my jeans and goose pimples started popping out all over me, for my ears had caught the plaintive, far-off whistle of a train: "Whoo-oo-ooo-oo! Whoo-oo-ooo-oo!" It came, faint and woeful sounding, shimmering through the stillness of the night.

We knew it was the evening express that ran from Louisville to Indianapolis. Every evening it went whimpering across the valley and we'd hear it at our place. Tonight it was late. It usually carried three or four passenger cars. If it left the track so close to the river, the engine might go plunging into the water, taking some of the cars with it.

"We've got to stop that train before it gets here," I declared.

"But how can we? The men will see us."

My brother was shaking with fright and I was too.

The two on the track had stopped their scraping and pounding and now stood surveying their work and muttering to each other.

"Come on," I whispered. Covered by the timber, we crept past them until we were sure they couldn't hear us. Then we started running down the track.

"How are you going to stop them?" Ricky panted.

"Fire!" I gasped, trying to catch my breath.

We must have run almost a quarter of a mile when the track began to turn, bearing to the left. If we could make it around the bend, the timber would hide us from the men behind. But we had no time to spare. We had just rounded the curve when we heard the rails singing and then we caught the faint clicketty-click of the wheels marking time down the track.

Quickly, we scooped up some dead underbrush and dry leaves and set a match to the heap. In a moment, the flames were leaping and snapping, while we gathered more brush to feed the fire. Far down the track, we could now see the headlight of the engine searching us out, and again the lonely whoo-oo-ooo-oo! who-oo-ooo-oo! came mournfully through the night.

We stood beside the track in the firelight, waving our arms and shouting, while the monster bore down on us. On and on it came, the whoo-oo-ooo-oo! now a thunderous shrieking in our ears. The train was almost upon us. "They're not going to stop," Ricky cried.

And, for a moment, I thought he was right. But the engineer had seen us and the train was slowing down.

Then, suddenly, we were seized from behind. Two rough-looking men, with bandannas over their faces, dragged us, screaming and struggling, down the embankment and into the timber's edge. Cursing and swearing, they stood us up against a tree and wrapped a rope around us, binding us to the tree. One of the men threatened us. "You young ones make one sound and you'll wish you hadn't," he snarled.

The other was already halfway up the bank to the tracks. "Come on, Gip," he called impatiently. "We've no time to waste. The young ones can't do any more harm."

We heard the train puffing and groaning, as it came to a stop. Then, there was the sound of scuffling, mingled with yells and shouts and the screams of women, as the masked men boarded the train. There was no doubt about it; they were going to rob the passengers.

In their haste, the robbers hadn't tied us up as well as they would have done if they had had more time, and after some minutes of wriggling and squirming, we managed to free ourselves.

Through the train windows, we could see the men going through the cars, taking the passengers' money and other valuables, while we stood in the clearing along the tracks, helplessly looking on.

Ricky started whimpering. "What can we do, Chub? Oh, what can we do?" he groaned.

Right then, there didn't seem to be anything that we could do. The people on the train were too frightened to help themselves. The robbers had guns too, and we didn't have anything to fight with; not anything at all! Or did we?

I caught my breath, and my heart almost leaped out through my collar, as suddenly I remembered the can of red pepper in my pocket. "We can do something! We can, Ricky," I cried. "I'll throw pepper in their eyes and you trip them as they come down the steps. Then, when they fall, we'll whack them with our sticks."

"But the pepper will blind them," Ricky objected.

"Only for a little while," I said. "And, besides, we've got to do something. Those people on that train are being hurt too."

Excitedly, we ran to the timber's edge and found a long stick and two shorter ones. Ricky took the long one, while with my knife, I pried the lid from the can of pepper and poured half of it into my cap. The robbers were working toward the back of the train. We crouched in the shadow by the steps of the last car and waited.

It seemed like a long time before we heard them coming. I nudged Ricky. "Get ready with your pole," I cautioned.

He moved it a little. "I am," he whispered.

My hands were shaking so I could scarcely hold the half-filled can of pepper and my cap, but I knew I had to carry out my part or we'd get caught. In that event, the robbers would probably kill us.

Now we could hear them warning the passengers to remain in their seats and be quiet. We knew they were waving their guns and backing out on to the rear platform. We knew too that, coming out of the lighted car, they'd be half-blinded in the darkness.

They were outside now. The door to the car slammed shut and the man called Gip started down the steps. His foot was reaching for the top one, when suddenly I jumped up and dashed the half can of pepper in his face. At the same time, Ricky poked the pole between his legs. He went down with a heavy thud, screaming and cursing.

The second man was close behind. Before he realized what was happening, he let out an oath and started down to help Gip, when his dose of red pepper hit him full in the face. Ricky's pole tripped him, and he fell heavily on top of his companion.

We didn't take time to whack the robbers. We bounded up the steps yelling for help. "We've got them down!" we cried.

With the conductor and several of the men passengers, we scurried back. Both robbers, blinded by the pepper, were going around in circles, tearing at their eyes, cursing and swearing. Their guns lay on the ground. The conductor scooped them up and took charge of the prisoners. The engineer and fireman were found tied up beside the track, and freed.

The train crew and some of the passengers gathered around us, patting us on the back and asking questions. We told them about the spike between the rails, and they took our names and asked us where we lived. Then the train backed up slowly into the Hawpatch station, some four miles away.

A week later, Father came home one evening with a long envelope addressed to Ricky and me. Inside was a letter from the president of the railroad company, praising us for saving the train, and a check for one hundred dollars made out to both of us.

We stared at the letter, and suddenly the lamplit living room wasn't big enough to hold us any more. We went outside into the starry darkness, and just stood there listening to the night wind whispering through the maples and smelling the sweetness of white clover washed with dew.

And presently we heard the far-off lonely whoo-oo-ooo-oo, as the evening train went whimpering across the valley once again.

Ricky reached for my hand and squeezed it. "I'm glad we took the shortest way home from Uncle Ben's," he said. And I was too.

13. ROBBERS' CAVE

One of Grandfather Bonifield's favorite stories was about the Robbers' Cave in the Hawpatch. According to Grandfather, the robbers had used the cave for storing their loot, way back when he was a boy. He never would tell us just where it was, and he warned us if ever we found it, not to go inside, for we might get lost. "A cave's no place for boys," he insisted, when we begged him to tell us where it was.

Then, one afternoon, Ricky and I came upon it while we were hunting for blackberries some two miles from our place, back along the creek in heavy timberland. We'd never have found it except that the water in the creek was low and we were down in the river bed instead of up on the bank. The cave was just a big gaping hole in the rocky side of the river bank, with a mouth big enough to drive a wagon through.

"Let's go in," I suggested, and, as usual, Ricky echoed my words.

"Let's," he agreed.

We stood in the entrance, peering into the darkness inside until we could see a little better. Then we went in to look around. The cave looked to be some twenty feet wide, but we couldn't see how far back it went. In the light from the entrance, we could see some bones scattered about; big bones that might have been those of a calf or a sheep. It was plain that some large animal had eaten his dinner there—perhaps, many dinners.

"What kind of animal do you suppose it was?" Ricky asked nervously.

"I don't know," I said, "maybe a bear or a panther."

"Or a pack of timber wolves," Ricky added ominously.

I started for the opening. "Come on," I said, "let's get out of here."

"Wait!" Ricky grabbed my arm and pointed. "There's a hole in the side wall," he cried excitedly.

I looked. Sure enough, in the wall of the cave, next to the floor was a hole big enough for us to crawl through. A shaft of light from the entrance seemed to be pointing it out to us.

I shuddered inside, but my curiosity was stronger than my fear. "Let's make us a torch and see what's on the other side," I said. We ran outside for some pieces of dead wood and soon had one lit for a torch. With the light from the firebrand, we could see that the hole opened into a small tunnel, some six feet long and just big enough for us to snake through on our stomachs.

I tried crawling through with the torch ahead of me, but a draft from the other end of the passage blew the flame back in my face and I had to give it up. I backed out and handed the torch to Ricky. "I'll crawl to the end of the tunnel and light a match to see what's on the other side," I told him.

But, when I lit a match, the draft from inside the cave promptly blew it out. After several attempts, I managed to keep the tiny blaze alive by shielding it with my hand. In the dim light, I could see that the floor of the inside room was level and appeared to be dry. I couldn't see what was in the shadows that dropped away beyond the tiny circle of match-light, but I did see something that started my heart thumping against my ribs.

Almost within reach of my hand stood a huge old trunk. It would have taken a dinosaur to have kept me from going in then. I squirmed out of the tunnel into the inside room, yelling to Ricky about my find. I had to crawl back through the passage part way to get the torch. Then my brother wriggled through, bringing more dead wood for torches. We stuck our firebrand in the sand and tackled the trunk.

It was half buried in the sandy cave bottom. The top was covered with dirt and the hinges were all rusted. We tried to raise the lid, but it was locked down and, in spite of the rust, the lock held.

"It must be an awful old trunk," Ricky said. "Maybe it's part of the robbers' loot."

I was thinking that too and wondering just what we'd do with the money, in case it was filled with old coins, but I didn't say anything. I was too busy trying to get inside. We worked and worked, but we couldn't budge the lock. Ricky crawled through the opening and rolled in a big rock ahead of him, to try to break the lock, but it wouldn't break. He went back outside again for some very stout sticks. We whittled one down to a wedge on the end, and tried to pry the top loose, but it wouldn't pry.

We stood there looking down at the old trunk and wiping the sweat from our faces. Ricky was almost in tears and, to tell the truth, so was I. The trunk looked like it was ready to fall to pieces, yet it held on to its secret like an old miser clutching his gold.

"We'd better go," I said reluctantly. "It must be about time to do the chores and Father will be looking for us. We'll come back tomorrow and bring a hatchet and something to pry the lid off."

Ricky shook his fist at the trunk. "I bet we'll get inside you tomorrow," he fumed. "I just bet we will."

He had just started to crawl through the passage when I heard him cry out. "Chub! Chub! It must be dark outside. There's no light coming through the tunnel." He backed out, looking scared.

"Oh, it can't be," I argued. "We haven't been in here that long, I know."

"But there isn't any light," Ricky persisted. "Look for yourself."

I was really alarmed now. I stuck my head in the passage way. Sure enough, my brother was right. There was only blackness ahead.

My heart beat a thubdy-dud-dub. What if we couldn't get out?

"I'm going to see what's the matter," I said.

"Maybe it is dark out. Maybe we have been here longer than I thought."

I wriggled into the passage and slid along on my stomach, feeling ahead for the opening. Suddenly my hand came up against something warm and fuzzy; something big—big enough to cover the hole! The hole through which we had to crawl to get out of the cave!

I started to scream but managed to choke it back. Quickly, I pulled in my hand and wriggled backward to the inside room. "Ricky," I said, trying not to show how scared I was, "there's some big animal up against the hole, covering it all up. I think it's a bear."

Ricky's eyes were wide with terror. "What'll we do, Chub? What'll we do?" he wailed.

"We've got to get him out of there," I said matter-of-factly, though I was quaking inside. "Maybe we can poke him with a stick and make him move."

"That'll make him mad," Ricky objected, "and even if he moves, we won't dare try to get past him."

"Let's move him first," I said boldly. "Then, we'll see about getting out."

My words seemed to reassure Ricky, and, although I was just as scared as he was, they sort of reassured me too. Being scared was one thing and doing something about it was another. Now that we knew what danger we were facing and had a plan to carry out, I felt a little braver. I took one of the heavy sticks and crawled back through the tunnel to poke the fuzzy monster. But, no matter how hard I poked, he wouldn't budge.

My heart settled down on my stomach with a thud. Cold sweat broke out all over me. It trickled down my face and down my back, while everything inside me was like a chunk of ice. Whatever it was out there blocking our way was just like the old trunk, I thought, stubborn and determined. I had no way of knowing for sure what it was, or how long it might keep us there. We were trapped, and there wasn't a thing we could do. Nobody knew where we were. I remembered Grandfather's warning, and for once I agreed with him that a cave is no place for boys. How I wished we had heeded his words.

I wriggled back into the inside room. There was no use now pretending I wasn't scared. I was. "Ricky," I sobbed, "we can't get out. He won't budge; we're trapped!"

My brother was shaking like an aspen leaf in the wind, but now he tried to cheer me up. "But, Chub," he quavered, "any animal will have to get up some time. He can't just stay there always. We'll wait till he goes out and then we'll crawl through. Anyway, Father's bound to come looking for us, when we don't come home."

"But he doesn't know where we are," I cried. "Even if he found the cave with the bear inside, he wouldn't know about the inside room."

We huddled together on the sandy floor of the cave in the flickering light of our firebrand. The old trunk, with its secret still locked inside, stood like a somber ghost watching our misery. It seemed to be mocking us. And sud-

186

denly I hated it with all the fury of my hope-lessness.

I picked up the big rock and hurled it with all my might at the old chest. The force of the blow shoved the trunk a little to one side. I walked over and kicked it. And then I noticed something I hadn't seen before; a crack along the lower edge had been hidden by the sand. Now it was showing.

We stuck the wedge in the crack and pried. The top of the trunk came away, leaving the bottom pasted in the sand. There was nothing at all inside. And, right then, I didn't care. All I wanted was to get out of that horrible place. But how could we, with a bear cover-ing the hole and no other way out? Or was there another way?

All at once, I thought of something I should have thought of before. "Ricky," I said, "that's a big old trunk. It never came through that hole. There must be another entrance."

Ricky jumped up. "That's right," he cried. "That's where the draft's coming from."

We started toward the back of the cave,

carrying our torch. It was the last one we had. When it burned out, we would be in total darkness, unless we could burn the trunk. We hadn't gone more than a dozen yards when the cave floor took a downward slant and then the passageway branched out in two directions. No draft came through from either corridor. "The draft must be coming in from some hole in the wall," I said.

Ricky was ahead of me, carrying the torch. He stopped short. "We can't go on," he declared. "We'll get lost and nobody'll ever find us."

With dragging feet, we turned around and went back to the trunk.

I looked through the tunnel again. It was still blocked. We hunkered down on the sandy floor and cried like a couple of babies. "We'll never get out of here," Ricky sobbed.

My brother's hopelessness roused me from my own fears. I patted his shoulder. "Aw, we will too," I insisted, although I was sure that we wouldn't. I wracked my brains for some means of escape. What did we have that we could use to make that bear get up?

We had nothing at all but our jackknives, the big rock, the trunk, and the firebrand. The firebrand! Maybe that would move the bear! Maybe—

I jumped up, grabbed the torch and crawled into the tunnel. Holding the firebrand ahead of me, I snaked my way through to the end and thrust the flame against that mass of fuzzy, hairy warmth. I smelled the odor of scorched hair. The massive body stirred. I heard the clatter of stones as the huge form moved upward and away from the opening. I still couldn't see what it was. But then I heard a soft "Moo-ooo-oo," and I almost collapsed with relief. "Ricky," I cried, "it's only an old cow! She must have wandered in there to keep cool.

Quickly we wriggled through the tunnel to the outer room. We stood outside the cave in the early twilight, feeling foolish but mighty happy too. Never before had the pine trees smelled so good, and the shallow waters dancing along in the creek bed sang a lovely song: "Going home! Going home! Going home!"